ACCLAIM FOR JOSHUA FURST's

SHORT PEOPLE

"[A] charged debut collection. . . . Like children, each story has its own way of demanding the reader's attention. . . . Furst's attention to his characters, his allegiance, remains constant. There's real humor here, and terror, and an enormous sense of all that can be lost."　—*Chicago Tribune*

"Complex and compassionate . . . a literary and social force that challenges the preconceptions of what it is truly like to be a kid today."　—*The Hartford Courant*

"*Short People* is a remarkable collection of stories, a wide-ranging, unsentimental exploration of the lost worlds of childhood and adolescence, where the angles are all slightly askew and the logic is more rigorous than our own. These are scary, funny, brilliantly observed narratives; Joshua Furst is a terrific writer."　—Jay McInerney

"A subtle, richly textured book."　—*Daily Mail*

"[These] stories are must reading. . . . Joshua Furst has a real knack for these childhood and adolescent traumas; his stories capture this sensitive and often-forgotten time of transforming human experience."
　—*Richmond Times-Dispatch*

"Both stomach turning and heart wrenching. These powerful stories are unnerving and scary." —*The Boston Globe*

"Joshua Furst's debut collection is a book about childhood, not war, yet it has the feel of a letter from the front written to a soldier just graduating from boot camp and dreading what's to come. Its message is heartbreakingly mature: it doesn't matter what the conflict's about. Once the fighting has started, you have no choice but to see it through."
—Dale Peck

"Raymond Carver-esque. . . . Like fairy tales, Furst's fables are full of hazards and temptations." —*Newsday*

"Any one of these stories is enough to break your heart. . . . Joshua Furst's debut is both enjoyable and important. It succeeds not only in questioning the behavioral norms of America, but also in reawakening our understanding of what it feels like to be a child."
—*The Times Literary Supplement*

"Joshua Furst writes about the world of young people with a complexity and lack of sentimentality that is rarely, if ever, explored in American literature. To read these stories is to enter into some dark worlds, but the magic here lies in Furst's affection for his characters and, moreover, his almost parental desire for them to turn out okay. *Short People* is, at its core, a book about caring, and no one has taken more care than the author himself."
—Meghan Daum

"Arresting. . . . As chilling as ghost stories—which, as the penultimate story reveals, they are in a way."
—*The Observer* (London)

"[Furst] examines childhood and its discontents with utmost empathy, refusing to sentimentalize the harrowing process of growing up. . . . Wonderful, a reminder of the chaos of youth that makes you relieved you never have to go through it again."   —*Newcity Chicago*

"The tragedy for many of the children in Furst's stories is their inability to see beyond the frail boundaries of their own restricted domains. . . . Furst's prose is precise and controlled. He is very good on the anomalies and misnomers revealed from a child's perspective, and these stories amount to a powerful and moving commentary on our society's often cynical and contradictory attitudes to childhood."
—*The Daily Telegraph* (London)

"So filled with energy, the lively characters of these stories jump off the page into the room, and amuse, shock, and also touch the heart of the reader with all the spirit of bright young people discovering the heights and depths of an astonishing new world."   —David Plante

"Furst clearly hasn't forgotten what it's like to be a child, but he also has a rare adult perception for the child's inner life. His refusal to take a romantic view can be disturbing, but it's also profound and often funny."   —*The Herald* (Glasgow)

JOSHUA FURST

SHORT PEOPLE

A graduate of the Iowa Writers' Workshop, Joshua Furst is the author of several plays. He has been the recipient of a Michener Fellowship and the *Chicago Tribune*'s Nelson Algren Award. He lives in New York City.

SHORT PEOPLE

SHORT PEOPLE

STORIES

Joshua Furst

Vintage Contemporaries
Vintage Books
A Division of Random House, Inc.
New York

FIRST VINTAGE CONTEMPORARIES EDITION, OCTOBER 2004

The following stories were originally published in slightly different form:
"Red Lobster" in the *Chicago Tribune* and
"She Rented Manhattan" in the *Crab Orchard Review*.

The Library of Congress has cataloged the Knopf edition as follows:
Furst, Joshua, 1971–
Short people : stories / Joshua Furst.—1st ed.
p. cm.
1. Children—Fiction. 2. Suburban life—Fiction. I. Title.
PS3606.U78 S48 2003
813'.6—dc21
2002035683

Vintage ISBN: 0-375-71407-3

Book design by Virginia Tan

www.vintagebooks.com

Printed in the United States of America
10   9   8   7   6   5   4   3   2   1

For

Janet, David and Melissa

Short people got no reason
Short people got no reason to live

—Randy Newman

Contents

SHORT PEOPLE

THE AGE OF EXPLORATION

It's summer, and when it rains the concrete smells sweet, slightly mineral, fresh. When it's sunny and dry, wavy lines hover over the asphalt. You have to wear shoes or you'll burn your feet. The neighborhood belongs to children, to chipmunks and ducklings, to things that haven't stopped growing. It belongs to Jason and Billy.

Billy is smart—he wears glasses. When he finds things, he learns what they are. He's older than Jason. Jason was born on April eleven, and Billy was born on January five. That makes Billy more than three months older. Jason and Billy are both six, but Billy will be seven first. Jason wishes that he were as old as Billy. Then he would know all the things Billy knows.

Billy knows what he's going to be when he grows up. A paleontologist. Not just somebody who knows about dinosaurs, a paleontologist is a searcher of the past, a finder of fossils, reader of bones and rocks, knower of what's hidden deep in the earth—ten million years deep; time is recorded in rings you can see if you dig deep under the blacktop. He has scoured the neighborhood, examined every rock and every chunk of bark in search of new fossils. Billy's favorite animal is the trilobite. It's a kind of an arthropod, a crab the size of a quarter, and it has a horseshoe shell. It's been extinct for hundreds of thousands of millions of years. He has one in his collection. He didn't find it, though; his father bought it for him at the museum. His other fossils he found. Footprints of a tiny bird. Petrified wood. A cluster of shells embedded in a piece of dolomite.

What does Jason know? He knows the routes to his favorite places. In one direction is the park with the concrete duck pond. In the other, the public pool. He knows which direction is which. He knows the shortcut you can take through the Evergreen Plaza parking lot if you want to go to the pool. He knows, when you walk to the park, that you have to walk on the grass and know where you're going because the sidewalk stops before you get there. Each time he goes exploring with Billy, the map in Jason's head gets bigger, but at the same time, everything already on the map takes on a greater variety of detail. He knows that the pool is east and the park is west. He's never been north or south, but he knows what they are and one day, hopefully, he'll go to these places. He might even go farther east past the pool, but he'll never go west past the park; after the park is the highway and you're not allowed to go across the highway.

Jason doesn't know what he wants to be when he grows up. Maybe a guy who works at the grocery story and tells you where to find marshmallow fluff. Maybe a lifeguard, like at the pool. Maybe unemployed, like his father, or an engineer, like his father was before. He won't be a paleontologist, though; that's Billy's job.

Billy knows, when you're at the pool, that you have to wait twenty minutes after you eat before you can go in the water again. Otherwise you get cramped up in your stomach. It's because of digestion.

The two of them sit on the scalding deck waiting for their twenty minutes to be up. They just ate Doritos. The other kids are playing. Not even the big kids are waiting for digestion, only Jason and Billy. Billy wishes he were a big kid, then he would've remembered that if you eat the Doritos the lifeguards sell at the snack stand you lose out on pool time. He would have known it's not worth it. He'll save the Starbursts he bought for the walk home. Billy is learning a bit about the world. He now knows to choose his temptations. The Doritos at the pool are always stale anyway.

What else does Jason know? Jason knows that the pool is always crowded. He knows where the invisible elephant lives by the fence. He knows that Doritos taste really good. He knows his phone number so if he's lost he can get a grown-up to call. He knows that the big kid with the white stuff caked on his cheeks, the one standing on the Jacksonville Jaguars blanket—see him, he's stretching his arms behind his head, flexing his muscles, yeah, that guy, with number 19 shaved on his head—he's going to dive off the high dive.

"No, he's not," Billy says.

"He is. I'll bet you."

"I'll bet you a dollar."

The big kid is walking now toward the diving part of the pool, but does that mean he's going to the high dive? He might be going to talk to the lifeguard, or find a girl he can throw in the pool. He might be looking for his friends to say it's time to go.

"That's too much," says Jason. "A quarter. Or okay, how 'bout a Starburst?"

"See, you're not sure."

"Yes, I am."

"Why won't you bet a dollar, then?"

"Look."

The kid's climbing the ladder. He's strutting down to the end of the board and turning back toward the metal hand loops. He's standing at the top of the ladder and staring out at the water. He's running, he's jumping, he's twisting in the air, tucking his one knee up, flexing his other leg straight. He's landing with a flop, first his foot, then his butt. An arc of water erupts like out of a shook-up soda can, shoots over the diving board, and splatters in the grass past the concrete, on the other side of the chain-link fence.

Jason knew. Jason won. "You owe me a Starburst."

"No."

"He dived."

"He didn't dive. He did that other thing, a what's-it-called."

"Same difference."

"No, you said dive and he didn't dive."

"I still knew he was going to go off the diving board."

"You didn't say that, though. You said dive."

"You knew what I meant."

Jason has yet to learn that thinking is private and speaking is public. To him, the words don't matter; it's what he meant that's really important. But Billy knows: say what you mean. He knows life is literal, even if that's a word he doesn't understand. The boy did a what's-it-called, not a dive. *That's* the truth. Ask anyone. Jason needs to learn what's real and what isn't. No one can hurt you if you know what's real and what isn't.

But Jason did know the boy would jump off the diving board. That part was true. "You knew what I meant," he says.

Billy didn't know what he meant, but he does now. He was corrected. He learned. Why does being friends mean that sometimes you have to be wrong even when you're right? "Okay, Jason, I'll let you be right. But I don't have to give you a Starburst, because the bet was about diving."

Jason knows how to sulk.

"Jason, I said you were right."

"You didn't mean it, though." Jason knows more than he seems to.

"Do you want a Starburst? Here. I'll even give you a pink one."

"No. I was right, though, right?"

"Yes. You were right."

"That's pretty cool that I could know what he'd do before he did it, though," Jason says. "It's magic."

Billy knows nothing is magic if you're a scientist. Scientists can find the reason for everything. That's their job. But then, scientists might be magicians, too. They know the secrets that make magic happen. No, they're scientists. Okay, but if nothing's magic, how did Jason know the boy would go to the diving board? Billy thinks and thinks, but he doesn't know.

Anyway, the twenty minutes are up. It's time to play and play and play. Until the pool closes for adult swim, and then it's time to leave.

Billy shares his Starbursts on the walk home.

In a pile of gravel, Jason finds a rock, a fossil with gouges and squiggles and stickie-outies that, even etched into dead stone, look like they were alive yesterday and might come to life again tomorrow. Jason feels weird. His map gets bigger, not in a normal way but up and down: down into the ground because that's where the fossil came from before it was part of the pile of gravel, and up toward the sky because he doesn't know why. Because finding fossils is something Billy does, not something Jason does. It seems not right. Jason collects bottle caps, not fossils. But then—and this is why the map gets bigger—if he found a fossil, which is Billy's job, how are he and Billy different?

Billy looks at Jason's fossil to make sure it's real. "Yup. That's a fossil," Billy says. "I haven't seen that kind before."

"So, do you don't know what kind it is?"

"I can find out in my books."

"Do I have to let you have it for that?"

Billy twists his lip up inside his teeth while he thinks. Billy is always thinking in between what you say and what he says back to you. "Yeah."

"But then you'll give it back?"

Billy ponders, but a thought comes to Jason like magic. "No, you know what, it's better if you have it to have in your collection." Magic because Jason knows it's the same thing Billy was thinking. "But you have to tell me what it is."

"I told you, I don't know."

"Yeah, but when you do."

Billy won't forget. He'll find out everything there is to know about Jason's fossil. Billy's good at things like that.

Jason's good at other things, like having magic thoughts.

The things Jason's good at are kid things. He's good at feeding the invisible elephant. The elephant eats right out of his hand. It rubs its long snout against his forehead, wraps it around him and pulls him close. It pokes at his belly with its thick tongue, tickles him. Its snout is wet like his kitty cat's nose. Its tongue is a very strong muscle that helps it eat and talk and spit. Sometimes it picks Jason up and throws him sprawling into the water. If it wanted to it could drink the pool empty and still be thirsty. Jason shows the elephant to Billy, but Billy can't see it.

"He's not an it, he's a him, and of course you can't see him. He's invisible. Look, though. I take the invisible peanut out of my pocket and hold it like that, and the elephant bends down like that and like that. See? He's eating."

Twisting and cavorting, Jason gets Billy laughing so he can't stop, so he's on his back on the cement. "It goes like that, and like that, and like that." Billy can see the elephant now. It might be invisible, but it's real, too. He won't admit it, but Jason can tell: he wouldn't be laughing if it wasn't real.

Jason's good at making Billy laugh. Jason's good at being silly.

Billy would deny it, but he wishes he were as silly as Jason. Life can't be all books. You have to go out and play sometimes. Playing is painful. Without any rules, Billy might get it wrong. Playing is like dreaming in front of other people. Billy only dreams when he's alone. He dreams that he's ten million years old and has watched the fishes crawl out of the sea, that he taught the apes how to speak, that he took the Cro-Magnon men hunting and caught a woolly mammoth. He's embarrassed by his dreams because they aren't true. Billy can't understand Jason. Jason dreams constantly, even in public. He doesn't care if other people laugh at him. He makes up what he doesn't know and believes so strongly in what he makes up that it almost doesn't matter that it's not true. It doesn't matter to Jason. It matters to Billy, though. How can Billy, after being needled—"Come on, it's your turn to come up with a game, it's not fair if I have to do everything"—to the point at which, daring himself not to be scared, he finally says, "Okay, let's play Stone Age," then go on a hunt for a dragon instead of a mammoth? There weren't any dragons in the Stone Age. There weren't any dragons ever— they're make-believe. It's silly. Billy feels foolish. But here he is crouching behind a park bench, crawling on his hands and knees.

"That's not a dragon, Jason, that's a bunny."

"No, it's a dragon disguised as a bunny," and somehow this makes sense when Jason says it.

Now Billy's running after the dragon, actually afraid that he might get burned if he lets it breathe on him. The dragon darts away—or did it fly? Jason says he saw its wings pop out, but who knows. Anyway, they've saved the world. They spin in circles and gaze at the sky until they're so dizzy they fall to the ground. Now Billy's grinning and flat on his stomach, exhausted and happy and feeling the prickle of grass on his skin, the clumpy soil, the breeze cutting over his sun-flushed body. The dragon got away. One day it will come back, but that's okay. Right now they're safe. How can he have so much fun? He doesn't know, but he can—with Jason he can.

Then when he gets home, he can't again.

They play Billy's games, too, sometimes, not really games but experiments. That way if anyone tells him he's being immature he can say, "No, I'm not, it's scientific." Who can hold his breath the longest underwater? Jason. Who can do the most somersaults in a row underwater? Jason. Okay, backward somersaults? Jason. Who can swim the farthest along the bottom of the pool before coming up for a breath? Jason. Who can jump off of the side of the pool and kick the most times in the air before he lands in the water? Jason again. Jason is better at playing than Billy.

Just look at him, scraped and scabbed, band-aids everywhere

from when he flew off that swing, when he took that quick turn on his Big Wheel and it tumbled over him, from the time he waded into the duck pond and slipped on the algae-caked concrete. Jason's a rubber ball; he'll bounce off anything. Billy is scrawnier, bony, pale, tender. He could fit one and a half of himself inside Jason. Winner games are no fun. Even when Billy comes up with the game, he loses. What would it be like to be like Jason, to jump really high and run really fast and believe in make-believe things?

How about this: who can jump into the pool backward and get closest to the edge without hitting it?

"You have to pretend there's an edge right behind you, too, like you're jumping into a tiny crack in the ground and if you can fit you'll go to the Fish Kingdom and grow gills and what else, Jason? I can't think what else."

"You'll be like a Fish God and all of the fishes will follow you around and talk bubble words to you and stuff like that."

"Yeah, stuff like that."

Billy goes first, a flat-footed slice nowhere near the edge. Then it's Jason's turn, Billy's turn, Jason's turn, Billy's turn. They incrementally tighten their descent, closer and closer to the cliff of white concrete. The rough bumps and holes look huge from an inch away, like they'd hurt if you hit them. As the wall slides past you feel a swoosh of wind. Every jump is a potential smashup. Billy's afraid he'll be scared to slice closer.

"And there's monsters with sharp teeth behind you. They keep coming closer. You have to be really tight to the wall or they'll bite you."

That's a Jason thought, silly and unrealistic, but Billy thought it. Billy said it. Maybe he *can* be like Jason. Maybe the world is more mysterious than science can ever explain. This must be what it's like to be Jason, unrestrained by the rules of reality, closer and closer to pure imagination. Billy relinquishes his questions why, his rules of logic. Closer and closer to the edge of the pool. Fear is the knowledge of danger. Billy, who has lived in fear since he can remember and has buffered himself against it with facts, suddenly and arbitrarily now discovers another, a preferable way. Imagine that you're indestructible. Then when you pound your chin on the cement, when blood stains the water and your jaw throbs, you won't care. Imagine yourself a winner. Billy, the frail, the once frightened, calmly walks to the lifeguard stand.

He grins. So this is what it feels like to be at one with the world. Four stitches. A scar to last a lifetime.

Billy and Jason—grass-stained, kool-aid-tongued, starbursting in a limitless world—smear dandelions across their cheeks and foreheads, their forearms. They climb trees and pick crab apples, which they then whip at each other like darts. Nothing can harm them. They scratch at welts and scrapes and scabs that appear on their bodies in places that they don't remember banging. Billy leans way back on the teeter-totter and suspends Jason high on the other side, holding him hostage until Jason tells him that being up there in the air is more fun than squatting and straining for leverage way down on the ground, at which point Billy slides off the edge and watches Jason bounce on the dirt. Or they hang from the monkey bars and turn the world upside down. Sometimes they play less rambunctiously. They overturn rocks and expose the Byzantine villages bustling with ants underneath; they drop pebbles on roadways and crumble bridges, careful not to hurt the ants, less interested in destruction, in their own ability to destroy, than in the construction that they provoke, in the mystery of creation. They sit and they spin and they spin, and they don't ever come when they're called. They don't even hear adult voices, not now. It's summer. Grown-ups don't exist in summer, not really.

Billy knows about the past and the present, but Jason has learned something new. It's a secret. Jason knows that the world gets bigger, but it gets smaller, too. He knows there are things he does not want to know. He knows his dad was an engineer once, and now he's an unemployed. He's going to be an inventor after summer is over and move the family away to a new city, Jason knows that too, but he can't tell anyone. Jason knows about the future, now. You can be one thing and another and then another and another and on and on, but the things you become sometimes wash the things you once were away. Jason knows what he wants to be when he grows up: he wants to be friends with Billy.

Jason is younger than Billy. But Billy lags behind as they walk to the park, shuffle-steps, falls over his two feet trying to keep up.

Billy, too, has a secret. He spills it when they reach the park. The fossil Jason found isn't a fossil. The museum people looked at it and said it was just a rock. Billy protested, defended Jason, said, "Yes it is, look at the squiggles and gouges like something scratched it," but they told him these markings could have been caused by anything, friction, a pickax, a Caterpillar.

"Do you want it back?" Billy asks.

"No."

"Well, what should we do with it?"

"I don't care."

Scientists should be dispassionate, but Billy is sentimental. He puts the rock back in his pocket. He wants it to be special even though it's just a rock. He wants meaningless things to have meaning. He's starting to suspect that he doesn't like all this learning about the world. He's starting to falter, to be less sure of the protection he thought he could find in science. He doesn't know this is what he's thinking—the subconscious is 687,500 bits faster per second, immeasurably smarter than the conscious mind, science has proved this—what he knows is he's no longer sure what he wants to be when he grows up.

Jason and Billy, awkward and quiet. Billy doesn't know why. Jason does, but he's forgetting it, trying to. Maybe then he'll be able to stay here. If you can imagine it, it can be true. If you can forget it, it's gone. If Jason can make right now be forever, the future will never come. That would be good magic. But there's bad magic, too. Like the way, even though they're best friends, Jason and Billy are weird with each other today. Why do things change without anything changing? Some bad witch blew toad dust on Jason and Billy and made them different than they were before. If Jason could be a magician, he would fight the witch, he'd boil a pot full of gooey things, old rubber bands and melted crayons, and he'd chase the witch away.

Maybe that's the witch there, pretending to be a mommy duck. She's leading her children on a tour of the concrete pond. They straggle behind her, and how do they know to form a V like that?

"I don't know," says Billy.

"Hey, Billy, you know what else? That mommy duck? She's a mean witch."

If Billy believes him, the future will change. They'll be Jason and Billy exploring the eternal present again. Jason and Billy, alive and thriving, restrained only by the limits of what they can think of. The duck's looking at them. She knows.

"And she's casting a mean spell on us right now."

"She's just a duck."

If Billy won't believe, there's no way they'll conquer the world. But if Jason believes that Billy believes, eventually Billy will stop trying to think—just for a moment—and see. The duck is a witch. Meanwhile, Jason goes searching for pebbles on which to cast his own anti-witch spells. They're hard to find along the edge of the concrete. He roots around in the tall weeds.

·"Billy, help me look for pebbles."

"No. I don't feel like it."

"How come?"

"I just don't."

Here's one and here's one and here's one and there's one. A handful of pebbles, no help from Billy.

"Eben-ku-deeben-ku-dooben-de-beetle-boo." He casts a spell on the pebbles, then throws one at the ducks. It plops in front of them and they chase after it, craning and lunging, mouths open. The mother duck, too. The pebble is a hunk of poisonous bread. Jason is feeding them, tricking them, saving Billy and himself from the future. He lobs another one. Another. Another. The ducklings crawl over each other to get at the bread. After they eat enough, Jason is sure, they'll get scared, for no reason, and run away. The mommy duck will go poof—Billy will see—and turn into the witch she is. Then she'll swim away, too, and take Jason and Billy's weirdness with her. It's magic.

"Look, Billy. Lookit, they're eating the pebbles."

Billy won't admit he's fascinated. He pretends he's bored, flips the rock that isn't a fossil from hand to hand, trying to look like he isn't looking.

Jason sings a song he knows they both like. "John Jacob Jingleheimer Schmidt, his name is my name too."

Billy feels like he's forgotten where he put something, but he doesn't know what that something is. He wonders, hey, why not sing along? Because he can't find the thing he can't remember. He has to keep searching until he finds it. He wishes he weren't in a bad mood. Look at Jason with ants in his pants, maybe he's not faking it, maybe he's just like this, maybe his life is simple and sweet. Billy wishes he knew Jason's secrets.

"Whenever we go out, the people always shout—come on, Billy, sing—there goes John Jacob Jingleheimer Schmidt."

But no, it's a stupid song. If that were his name, he wouldn't be Billy. It's scientific. And he can't be Jason, either. Anyway, he doesn't want to be Jason anymore. Jason's changed. Jason is no longer silly, he's fake silly. Okay, he *is* still silly, but doesn't he know that sometimes you have to be sad?

"Stop it, Jason."

"No. I don't have to." Jason sings louder. "John Jacob Jingleheimer Schmidt, na na-na na-na na-na . . ."

The ducks watch and listen. Jason hops up and down, shouting the refrain. "John Jacob Jingleheimer Schmidt." He throws pebbles, one at a time. The ducks go wild, hungry for more.

Billy bites his lip. He covers his smile. Jason's a magician, drawing the joy out from inside of Billy, until finally, he can't hide his laughter.

"See, Billy? It's magic. You try."

The rock that isn't a fossil is slightly larger than a pebble; maybe an inch in diameter, thin as a skipping stone. It sails slightly higher and soars slightly farther than Jason's pebbles, then lands on the back of one of the ducklings. The duckling squawks. It swims in tight circles, flutters its wings. Its mother watches. Its siblings scatter. The rock sinks unnoticed below the surface.

"You didn't say the magic words."

"Did I hurt—is the baby duck okay?"

It fluffs its feathers, swimming in a wobbly line toward its mother. The duck is okay, shaken up but okay. Children need ten hugs a day. A kiss will make it feel better.

The boys are both silent. What do they know?

The mother duck is preening over her young. She smoothes down its feathers. She pecks at its shoulders, pecks and pecks. No kisses. She clamps her beak over its neck. No hugs. It bobs and struggles. A frenzy of batting wings, of splashing water. She's jerking her head. She's breaking its neck. A piercing, full-throated moan, and then the mother duck gathers her ducklings into formation, swims away with them, leaving the limp one behind; its soft belly and webbed feet glisten in the sun.

"Jason, we killed it."

"No, the mean witch killed it."

Summer is waning, the days growing shorter, not even magic can stop it from ending.

Jason tells Billy he's moving soon. School looms ahead, dark and ominous. Billy is scared of all he doesn't know. He's scared of what will happen after Jason's gone. The neighborhood reeks of bad science.

Jason rides off toward his father's new job. He twists in his seat belt and waves out the window. If you run at supersonic speed you can keep up with the car as it drives away, and you won't get tired even if you have to run for two and a half days without stopping except to get gas and go to the bathroom. Run, Billy, run. Come on, Billy, keep up. But Billy, the smart one, the older one, can't keep up. He veers off, sputters out on the side of the road. He huffs and he hunches. He waves.

Jason crosses the highway into the who-knows-where.

When he looks at his fossils, Billy sees Jason. He knows Jason's gone, though. You can't hold your friends forever in limestone. That would be magic. The fossils are boring now. The traces of life he finds in them are much too constrained, dull, dead.

Goodbye, Jason.

Billy is far away, like the park and the pool, the ducks and the pile of gravel, the big kids who can use the diving board, Evergreen Plaza and its parking lot, the asphalt, the concrete, the crab apples, the teeter-totter, the Big Wheels and bike trails, monkey bars, training wheels, dandelions, ants, east and west, north and south where he never went. The map in Jason's mind is useless now, but soon he will draw a new one. Who knows what will be on it. Buried treasure.

'Bye, Billy.

Delgado, BB

u32.3691465

There will be so much noise. As his parents walk him through the neighborhood—each holding one hand, sometimes they will swing him up off of the ground and he'll bicycle-kick in the air between them—boom boxes, car alarms, shouts, *hey, hey chulo, ou-u-u-e mamacita,* even the wind belting around tight corners, the hundreds and hundreds of sounds, will disorient him. The sounds will knock him off balance. They will surround him and he will shrink into himself to escape them. His parents' hands will be all he can rely on to guide him toward his home. Even once he's there in the shotgun where each piece of furniture is reliably fixed in place, where every sound is attached to a known source of emission, he will duck and cover and attempt to evade the barrage of noise. He will be forever trapped in an echo chamber where the sound gets louder the longer it bounces. The chatter, the bicker, the shout and gasp, the thud and the wince, all the ways that his parents communicate just how much they truly care about each other will ricochet unendingly, will box out so much space, that simply to stay out of the cross fire he will lie on the floor, under the kitchen table, his chin and his belly sweeping the linoleum. He'll wonder if it's true that because he can't see them, they can't see him.

THIS LITTLE LIGHT

Shawn Casper dons his new gray suit, clips on his one tie and rides in the back seat of the family Festiva toward the church, a pyramidal shed sided in brown aluminum that rises at steep, oblong angles; it looks like an immense arrowhead piercing the ground past the parking lot.

An usher takes him from his mother and father and leads him to a closet-sized annex behind the baptismal pool. The usher hands Shawn a plain white robe—a sheet cut with three holes, one for his head and one for each arm—then closes him into the darkness. The room has no windows, no switches, no bulbs.

After his eyes adjust, Shawn sees how spare the room is: one metal folding chair and a small shelf. He unties his brown faux-leather dress shoes. He removes his socks and folds them in half, laying each one in the heel of its corresponding shoe so he won't be confused, so the germs on his feet will stay separate. He strips off his suit, folding and refolding the jacket, slacks and shirt, aligning them in a neat stack on the shelf according to bulk, then spreads his tie flat across the top to give the appearance that it's still clipped in place. He leaves his underwear on. His scrawny body embarrasses him, and the thought of the whole congregation—his elders and peers, he's not sure which is worse—seeing his private parts terrifies him. Hoping his body transforms with his spirit, he shimmies into the white sheet and, minding his posture, sits on the cold chair to wait.

Goose bumps rise on his flesh. He closes his eyes, pinches his tear ducts, attempting to concentrate on Preacher Dan's sermon.

"I was reading my Bible the other day, thinking about how special this day is for our young friend, Shawn Casper, and I happened on a verse from Luke—Luke 3:22. Do you all remember that one?"

Shawn repeats the words in his head as they're spoken, tells himself, *Pay close attention, this is important,* but the desire to listen occludes comprehension. He catches a few phrases—". . . in bodily form like a dove. And a voice came from Heaven . . ."—and in trying to discern the mass of their meaning, he misses whatever comes next. Eventually the words stream past him entirely. His mind wanders toward more prosaic things: the itchy texture of the cotton robe, how hard it is to clip his cat Isaiah's claws, what it would be like to be color-blind. He starts counting things—rivets in the wall, the minutes until he will be born again.

For he is about to be accepted into the body of Christ. He is about to be saved from his suffering. He can't imagine what that will feel like. Will it be warm? Will he be like Jesus in every way? This is what he strives for. To Shawn, the world is either/or: either you're saved or you're not; either you're good or you're bad; like his father says, "Either you're part of the problem or you're part of the solution." Right now, and for the next twenty minutes or so, Shawn is part of the problem, the bad, the unsaved, locked alone in the darkness just like all those others who haven't accepted Christ into their hearts. A little over a year ago, his parents announced that he was old enough to make the decision that would define the rest of his life—whether or not to be baptized into the faith. They couldn't choose his path for him; the responsibility was his alone. They urged him to establish his own personal relationship with God before making up his mind, to speak with Jesus through prayer and listen carefully to what the Savior had planned for him. He prayed frantically, as per their instructions, but Jesus never answered. At church he had been told repeatedly that anyone who asked would be accepted into Heaven. Shawn was sure that he must be asking with an impure heart, must not mean it, because if he did, Jesus would say, "Welcome home, I have been waiting for you." Then, Shawn could say, "I am ready," and know he was telling the truth. Finally, in desperation and still with no answer, he requested his baptism, ready or not. His hope is that from this day forth, when he prays, Jesus will miraculously respond.

The door is opened, and Shawn steps humbly forward, his head down, his face red, out of the darkness and onto the stage. He climbs the portable stairs behind the water tank—as big as a coffin, glassed in on four sides—until he stands, terrified and exhilarated, on a thin, carpeted platform next to Preacher Dan.

He looks out into the congregation, finds his mother and father, holding hands. His mother waves at him. His father whispers something in her ear and softly pulls at her arm. She waves again, this time with a waist-high flicker of fingers. Shawn grins and blushes.

Behind him, Preacher Dan kneels in the water and whispers, "Lie prone, now. Relinquish your body into my hands." Preacher Dan is a vessel of the Lord. Quick with sympathetic nods and mild jokes, he carries an unassuming personality inside his beefy body, a protective authority that his parishioners trust absolutely. His hands are thick and calloused. Shawn lets them buoy and cradle his head. He breathes deep and bobs on the water's surface.

The question, the dare, "Do you, Shawn Casper, accept Jesus Christ as your personal Savior?"

"Yes."

"Are you, Shawn Casper, prepared to die with Christ, who in His infinite kindness sacrificed His life to save you from sin?"

"Yes."

With his right hand, Preacher Dan braces the back of Shawn's head. Preacher Dan is built like a football coach, barrel-chested, square-jawed; a sandy mustache cut perfectly straight partially masks a hairlip scar. With his left hand, he presses a towel over Shawn's mouth and nose. He squeezes his hands together around Shawn's head. Shawn can't breathe.

"I baptize you in the name of Jesus Christ, your Lord and Savior."

Submerged, Shawn clenches his eyes shut and waits for the change. Now that Jesus is about to arrive, Shawn wants to cement the misery and confusion of his past life into his heart forever. That way, when he's out planting seeds, he will know whereof he speaks. He tries to call to mind the totality of horror and fear he's felt in his nine years on Earth, but the chill of the water, the clamp of the towel, the second-by-second deoxification, all these things are over-whelming. He squirms. He is drowning. He knows, from years of public-pool competitions, the exact number of seconds he can go without a breath: thirty-two. To press his lungs further makes him dizzy. The blood rushes to his brain. He didn't think he'd actually *die*. His heartbeat echoes in his ears. His lungs burn and tremble. He doesn't want to *die*. He grasps at his face, but the preacher's thick arms are like boa constrictors — Shawn can't reach around them, the elbows block and overpower him. He kicks and splashes. His knees beat against the glass.

Jesus, please, if I die now, forgive me for all the sins I have done. Forgive me for not eating breakfast this morning — it was just because I was nervous. And forgive me for . . . for . . . You know what I mean, Jesus, everything, even the sins I can't remember. I'm so scared now, Jesus. Make me go to Heaven. Please, please, make me go to Heaven. All I wanted was to get baptized. Please, help me, God. A-men.

Shawn stops struggling and lets his body go limp. He can feel himself leaving it behind.

Then he is coughing and gasping, back on the surface. Alive.

"As you died with Christ, so you are born with Christ."

He gulps down air. Everyone claps and the shallow vibrato, the preprogrammed beat of the electric keyboard, starts in on Hymn 162. Wet needles of hair poke at Shawn's eyes, filling them with water every time he blinks. He flips the hair back with a jerk of his head and slaps at his ear, trying to pound out the sluicing, logged water. The laughter this elicits from the congregation humiliates him. He gazes out at them. Except for his mother in her Christmas dress and his father in his best tan suit, the parishioners are clothed in t-shirts and jeans, khakis and short-sleeved button-downs minus the ties, tank tops, tennis shoes, primary colors, logos and slogans for businesses big and small. They all look the same as they did before. Black tears weave clotted webs along his mother's cheeks. She wiggles her fingers at him again and beams. His father, chin in his chest, shakes his head at short intervals as if he's shooing a fly away; when he looks up—yes, Shawn knew it—his eyes are rimmed red; he nods once, a hard, taut expression on his face, the bitten lip betraying the pride it holds back.

Shawn wonders when the feeling of transcendence will kick in.

Preacher Dan hugs him and whispers, "A heck of a ride, huh?" before delivering him into the hands of the usher with a congratulatory wallop on the back.

At Camp Corinth, where Shawn spends one week each summer playing Frisbee golf and Red Rover and watching puppet shows about God's abundant love, he and his fellow campers revel in passing around warm fuzzies, homemade yarn Koosh balls that hang from strings, to be draped, with a hug, around each other's necks. Warm fuzzies, like God's love, are best when given away, but Shawn likes the warmth of receiving them better. He likes knowing that he's accepted and special. Preacher Dan has always seemed to embody the traits of a warm fuzzy, soft with love and humble understanding. Now Shawn sees something chaotic and tense roil under the calm on Dan's face. He wishes he could ask: *Why did you have to hold me down so long? Why did you have to clap me so hard on the back? Were you trying to hurt me?* But no one can question Preacher Dan.

Back in the dressing room, Shawn searches his body for physical changes. Here on his wrist is the mole by which his mother has always said she would identify him if he ever suffered a disfiguring accident. And here are the scrapes he received last week while riding his bike no-handed, the scabs white and spongy on his elbow now. His belly button is still an inny. The veins on the back of his hands run the same way they did before. Changing his clothes, he checks his thing and sees that it's still distressingly circumcised; he'd hoped that after his baptism it would start to look like his father's. He's the same. Nothing's changed. He's the same.

There must be a reason. He can only assume that he's somehow done something that even Jesus, who supposedly forgives everyone, can't forgive.

For a couple of weeks, Shawn despairs at his lack of transfiguration, but before this despair can shatter his faith, he makes a pact with himself: try harder, be better; only with perfection will Jesus talk to you. There is a right and there is a wrong and Shawn dedicates himself to rooting through all the morsels of his life, until he's rid himself of the bad bits. He imagines what would happen if he succeeded: God reaching down, placing a finger to Shawn's forehead, a radiant light spreading through his body, ascendance, briefly, then touchdown and a continued life of walking through a world that can tell he's a Christian by his vibrant love. On the first day of Advent, he helps his mother arrange the crèche. His father sets up the Jesse Tree, a spindly, dead-looking thing at the start, but as the days progress toward Christmas, it fills out with paper leaves. Each references a different Bible verse, with a short study plan on one side and a really well-done, three-color potato print that relates to the verse on the other. Shawn and his parents sit by the fire for an hour each night before dinner and study the day's lesson. His father reads the verse out loud and they, as a family, follow the study plan, answering the questions and extrapolating meaning from what before were just words.

"Why did God allow His people to fall into sin as they waited for Moses to descend from Sinai?"

"What can you do not to turn into a pillar of salt?"

"How should you react if God treats you the way He treated Job? Think of a moment in your own life when you felt like God was testing you with painful trials. Did you respond like Job?"

Shawn's father's eyes tear up as he grapples for an answer to the Job question. He flashes Shawn's mother a look full of trepidation, and she responds softly, all wide, caring eyes, silently cupping his hand between her palms, kissing the fleshy base of his thumb. He breathes deep and exhales through flapping lips, a lawn mower engine running out of gas.

"Shawn, now that you're baptized, I think you're old enough to talk about this. You know, I didn't used to be as good as I am now at providing for you and your mother."

"Uh-huh." Shawn is transfixed by the incremental separation of bark from branch as the log in the fire burns.

"Shawn, pay attention. Your father's telling you something important."

The bark curls in on itself as it pulls away from the hard wood underneath. It pulses orange and red, like it's breathing.

"Do you need a moment with the Lord?"

He tells himself to stop watching the fire.

"Shawn?"

His mother takes his father's hand again and squeezes. "Chad, he's paying attention now."

"Okay, I'm thinking about the story of Job and I'm thinking, when I was a kid—up through, Jeez, till I was twenty-three, twenty-four years old." He looks to Shawn's mother for help with the facts. "Twenty-four. The third one was when I was twenty-four. I was inside for my twenty-fifth birthday." She nods supportively. "All through that time, Shawn, I felt like Job. That's exactly what I felt like. I didn't handle it all that well, though. I didn't have any faith and I thought I had to do it all myself."

"You didn't have any faith, like you didn't believe in God?"

"That's right."

"You didn't believe in God?" Shawn's eyes bulge. His mouth hangs open.

"Listen, Shawn, it was a . . . I got in a lot of trouble."

"Like you were a Devil worshipper?"

"No. Well, in a way, but I didn't know it. The, uh, the Devil's minions, um, ran through my bloodstream, I guess you could say."

Shawn scoots in closer and peers at his father. "You worshipped the Devil?"

"I'm saying—"

"No, Shawn, your father did not worship the Devil."

"I'm saying I used to drink sometimes. And things like that."

The image of his father drinking is preposterous. Shawn slaps the floor. He rolls on the floor in laughter.

"Shawn, this is serious. This is the Jesse Tree."

"It wasn't a good thing. You're lucky, Shawn. You're lucky to have a father now who isn't—who can take care of you. The thing is, Shawn, there were—I was like Job. I felt like the whole world was out to get me, and there were some people whose love I really needed who didn't treat me all that well. And that's why I was destroying myself like that. Do you understand what I'm saying, Shawn?"

"Um . . . Uh-huh."

"I didn't know that I had Jesus to turn to."

"And you, Shawn, *do* know that you have Jesus to turn to."

"And you've got us and we love you."

"Did Jesus talk to you after you turned to Him?"

"Eventually."

Shawn beams.

"Have you ever felt like Job, Shawn?"

He can't remember. Nothing horrible has happened yet in his life. "I guess when I can't get Jesus to talk to me."

"Yes, that's like Job. Good, Shawn."

"What do you do when you can't get Jesus to talk to you?"

"I um . . . I keep listening anyway?"

This is the first of Shawn's correct Jesse Tree answers, and as the month progresses, he racks up more and more of them, making his parents proud and winning their approval of his wish not to receive gifts on Christmas—Epiphany is so much more appropriate.

Over the next year and a half, Shawn carries his copy of *The Way*—a gift from Preacher Dan, given ceremonially during his baptismal coffee hour—with him at all times, leafing through it when he sees something he doesn't like, the way others might look up a word they don't know in the dictionary. He judges, and finds wanting, most of what he reads in the *Record Herald*. During recess at school he shakes his head in disgust at the other kids chasing each other around the soccer field in flagrant display of evil Lust. He pounds tables and dashboards as if they are Bibles, rants until spit sprays out of his mouth, his face turning red, his ears burning.

Not even his mother escapes his scrutiny. When, for example, she carts him along to pick out a chair for the living room, she keeps rearranging their route through the store to bring them back to one particularly plush model, dusty rose with indented sky-blue stripes offset at intervals by puffy clusters of pale green-and-yellow flowers. She loves the chair even more than she loved last year's home splurge, the wall-to-wall heather-gray carpeting. She runs her fingers over the fabric—coy and guilty, daring, blushing like she's a little girl and not a very Christian one.

Shawn manages to wait until they're in the parking lot before exploding, but as they walk toward the car, his lecture begins.

"It's called covetousness, Mom. It's very, very, very, very bad.

You shouldn't covet your neighbor's wife. You shouldn't covet your neighbor's home. It's in *The Way*. The Ten Commandments. Those are sins, Mom. You sinned."

"I didn't sin, Shawn." Her voice is already weary and, Shawn thinks, distressingly indifferent given the gravity of what she's done.

As she starts the engine and pulls onto the access road, he fumes, struggling with ways to prove his point. "Because, even if you didn't play with the fabric and drool on it and stuff, God would have known you were sinning cause He can see all your bad thoughts. You coveted so everybody could see and that's . . . it's really bad, Mom . . . Isn't it really very bad?"

She watches the road as if he's not there.

"Mo-o-om?"

"Not right now, Shawn."

"It's a sin, though."

"You've already made it clear that that's how you feel."

"But, don't you care that it's a sin and you just did it and now God saw you sinning?"

"Shawn."

"And that now you're going to go to Hell?"

"Shawn, I'm trying to drive."

He leans forward as far as his seat belt allows, twisting in a fitful attempt to look her in the face. "You don't care?"

"Not right now."

"That's a sin too. That's an even bigger sin."

She taps the brake. "Now listen to me, Shawn." For a moment he's sure she's going to yell at him, but instead she swallows and, silently mouthing the words, prays, *God, make him stop*, before accelerating in silence.

"I'm listening, Mom. Mom? See, I'm right and you don't even care." His arms snap across his chest and he stiffens and glares at his reflection in the window.

For the rest of the day, he harumphs and sighs and stalks from one room to another, but every time he settles in, there she is, cheerfully trying to spoil his bad mood. He knows she's not really following him, that she's doing laundry and paying bills, writing letters and calling friends, but he's pretty sure that she chooses what to do when based on which room he's in. He sulks in the kitchen, and she comes and unloads the dishwasher. He sulks in the bathroom, she cleans the litter box. He sulks on the back porch, she hangs the linens, waving to him as she goes. The one room Shawn stays away from is his bedroom; what would be the point of brooding in there, where his mother couldn't see him nurse his anger. He sulks in the living room, leafing through back issues of *Family Life*, until she says, "Shawn, now I'm going to fold the laundry and watch *Days of Our Lives*, so you can stay or not, but if you stay, I want you to smile for me," and she roughs up his perfectly side-parted hair. By now, he's less upset with her for sinning than for being such a grown-up. Her unshakable cheeriness makes him feel childish, and that's not right—after all, she's the one who is wrong. He glowers at her from the couch for a while, but she watches her television show and folds his underwear and doesn't seem to care at all.

At dinner, Shawn politely declines his father's request that he say grace.

"Shawn." His father's eyebrows jackknife and Shawn knows he can't argue.

"God's great, let's eat. And make people be not so covetous. A-men."

"Thank you, Shawn."

Throughout the meal, Shawn clatters his silverware. Instead of eating he dissects his favorite made-from-scratch meatloaf. Nibbling a bit of the ketchup-glazed top, he proclaims that it tastes like soap.

"Shawn's had a bad day," says his mother, attempting to explain.

Preoccupied with the mound of margarine he's folding into his baked potato, his father doesn't look up from his plate. "Something on your mind, Shawn?"

"He's just angry at me. He'll get over it."

"No."

His father smirks. "No, you're not angry at her, or no, you won't get over it?"

Laughing, his mother says, "Both," and then launches into her side of the story: blah, blah, blah, blah and now she's getting the silent treatment.

Unable to endure any more slander, Shawn finally blurts out, "Not true! That's not how it was!"

"Oh? How was it?"

"The way she says it makes it sound all different than how it really happened." But before he can get the truth out, she laughs. Shawn tries to be Christ-like and keep his dignity as enmity gathers around him. "Dad," he says, "could you please ask Mom to stop laughing at me now?"

"She's not laughing at you. She just thinks you're cute."

With an attitude like this, Shawn is horrified to realize, his father might also remain with the camels and sinners, unable to squeeze through the eye of the needle when Judgment Day finally comes.

Please, Jesus, make Mom and Dad feel bad for being so mean. Make them know that I just want them not to go to Hell. Tell them I'm right and it's bad to covet and it's even badder to poke fun at me if they really love me which I think they don't. Cause, otherwise, why do they do things You don't like that might make it so that they won't go to Heaven? Make them please be better so I don't have to be mad at them. Thank You. A-men.

Throughout the rest of the meal, his parents chat about the chair, what it looks like, where to put it, did she get a deal. Refusing to eat is the only expression of protest Shawn makes. He shoves the food on his plate from one pile to another, building geometric sculptures with it, chopping the meatloaf, potato and broccoli into tiny fragments of fiber.

His father reaches over him to take a forkful from the pile.

"Remember the rule, Shawn. Don't take more than you're going to eat. Or else you have to sit here until it's gone."

He suffers the penalty glumly, all the more so because it's his mother who, as bedtime draws near, takes the plate away, scraping the cold landscape of mush into the garbage disposal and releasing him with a good-night kiss on the cheek.

The chair arrives at the house a week later. Shawn's mother loves it so much she decides not to take the plastic off, for fear that without it the fabric will wear thin and pick up stains, turning tawdry within the year.

To his consternation, Shawn likes the chair as well. Worse, as he enters puberty, urges he didn't know even existed start crawling inside him like viruses. He knows they're sins—virtuous thoughts don't make him feel clammy. Confused and afraid, and mostly ashamed, he carves God's rules deeper into his brain. He hoards and displays the parts of himself that exemplify his moral fiber. He fidgets and hovers over his good deeds, as if he's afraid they're going to break. He scares himself with Scripture. This is the Shawn for the world to see: Shawn the literal interpreter, for whom actions, thoughts and beliefs have palpable, cut-and-dried consequences; Shawn the trooper, who, beacon and map in hand, patrols his life and the lives of everyone else he knows, prodding the Evil out of the kingdom of Good; Shawn the player with action figures, who instead of staging intergalactic battles walks his dolls through the Passion, Crucifixion and Ascension of the Lord Jesus Christ. When he's able to sustain this level of intense devotion to the Christian life, Shawn knows God is walking beside him. But more and more often, God allows the Devil and his minions to intercede. They pluck him off of the gleaming prairie of God's country and carry him piggyback into dark places where Evil hangs in the air like car exhaust. Shawn breathes it in and becomes someone else. This Shawn steals snacks between meals. This is the Shawn who, at Camp Corinth, lies silent in his bunk, staring at the springs above him, and wonders if the defiant boys boasting about the girls they made out with, the girls whose breasts they touched in the woods, are lying. This is the Shawn who, wishing he knew what a girl's breast felt like, caresses his nipple until it's sore and inflamed. This is the Shawn who wishes to know that of which he condemns. The Shawn who, back home in bed, has been touching his thing, trying futilely to make it grow.

As if reading his mind, Shawn's mother leaves a book on his bed: *Wait . . . Until You Hear This: A Christian Kid's Guide to Sex.* The very first chapter explores the topic of onanism. It can make you crazy; if you do it long enough, you become addicted and unable to think about anything else and then you stop washing and stop getting haircuts and flies and worms and things start growing in your head and you finally stop wearing anything but long trench coats and gloves to cover the hairy warts on your hands, and there's a 97% chance that if you start out onanizing—it's also called self-abuse—when you're young, you'll become a dirty-magazine reader and a premarital sex offender and start showing your member to people you don't know on the street and this can escalate to things like rape and murder and serial killing. The book has examples, stories from real people who fell into the world of sex sins before they found Jesus and were born again. Shawn reads it so many times that the pages come unglued.

Still, late at night in his room, he can't stop the minions from pouncing on his bed and insisting that just one more time won't hurt. Put off righteousness till tomorrow, they say, tonight, they have something to show him. They remind him of the part in *Wait . . .* that describes in scientific terms what happens to you when you onanize. You're overcome with impure thoughts and your member grows heavy and firm with sex. Once the thoughts have taken complete control of your body and mind and soul, you enter a trance and your member rejects the sex from your being, leaving a gooey white stain on your hand. They remind Shawn that he's never seen this stain, he's never felt the sex take hold of his body, that all he's ever done is yank on his thing until it's chafed, red and bloated. Shouldn't he just once find out what he's missing? He tries to resist them. He protests, "It's a sin. I don't believe in sinning." They laugh at him. They say that it's a sin because it's such fun, he'll see. The stauncher his will, the more conniving the minions become. They open *The Way* to the Song of Solomon. What are those vineyards in bloom? They ask. Can you imagine them? He can and he does. They wear down his will. Don't you want to arouse and awaken love? This is the Bible, they remind him, that makes it okay. Can't you see those two breasts like fawns? Come, browse among the lilies. He reaches down and his beloved— whoever she is—dances blurry and half-formed in the olive grove of his imagination. He lets her kiss him and massage him and other things that get hazy because he's not sure what they are. He lets himself study the way his thing changes shape. It grows and shrinks and grows and shrinks. Later, when he's exhausted and all that's come out are clear little teardrops that thread like corn syrup on his finger when he touches them, he wonders if he made the stain. He flips through *Wait . . .* in search of the description. He knows he's failed—in God's eyes and Satan's—because he's sinned, but not even correctly, the wrong stuff came out, he's still doing it wrong. And he lies awake, feeling unclean and inhuman, wishing he could die instead of sinning like this. Wondering what God does to sex addicts like him. Terrified of the rapist serial killer he will become when he grows up. Promising God yet again that if He forgives him, just this one more time, it will never happen again. That's lying, too. It gets so bad that one night—a night when he is actually able to resist, though in order to do so, he has to make a rule that his hands stay above the covers—he wakes up with teardrops all over his underwear.

Convinced that if he doesn't change his ways soon, his chances at a conversation with Jesus—forget getting into Heaven—will be lost forever, Shawn reads the Christian comic books from Shepherd's House and listens to *Small One* and *The Kids' Praise Album* and the whole Monarch collection of children's records that teach the Fruits of the Spirit and the Ten Commandments and the Seven Seals of the Apocalypse. He asks himself, about once every minute, What Would Jesus Do, though with no word from the Man Himself, he never comes up with an answer. He tells himself it's not too late, that if he does everything so right that he becomes the rightest person on Earth, God might still catch him in the floodlight He uses to peer into people's souls and say to Himself, "Gosh, that boy, Shawn Casper, he's really something. Look at him, Saint Peter. Moses, come see this. He's only in fourth grade and he's already the best Christian ever. You don't see him? Right there. The one with the halo. I'm shining My light on him. It tickles Me all over when I see a kid like that."

But Shawn knows he's no longer a kid like that.

On Wednesdays, the Casper family's busy day, when Shawn's mother and father both go straight from work to their evening meetings—he's on the church council, she's in the choir—Shawn rides his bike home from school to the house he must inhabit until nearly bedtime, long after dark, alone. He tries to remember that God will protect him, but each Wednesday as he pedals slowly home, he remembers the Wednesday last week, when he hid in the hall closet, or two weeks ago, when he cowered in the shower staring at his hands, or the one before that, when he curled in a ball beneath the covers of his parents' bed and cried. He remembers all the Wednesdays since his parents stopped hiring sitters last year, each one so much like the others—him shivering, shaking, afraid of he knows not what. Each new Wednesday picks up where the last one left off. The minions just keep getting stronger.

Please Jesus, please let me get through this hump day without doing anything to make You mad at me. I promise I won't watch the TV shows Mom and Dad don't like me to watch. I won't turn the radio to the bad stations. If You please help me, I won't do anything wrong. Let me not have the bad thoughts that I sometimes have. Let me pass through the darkness and into the light. And, Jesus, can You let me not be scared, never again? Thank You, Jesus. A-men.

This Wednesday, the minions are especially active. And worse, Shawn suspects his father of conspiring with them. Last night, even though he gave up smoking for Lent and promised this time it would be for good, Shawn saw him sneak a cigarette out in the garage. How could he do this? It's horrible! Not only does smoking disappoint God, but to make a promise and then break it is basically the same as lying. It's a big sin, and Shawn's father didn't seem apologetic or remorseful at all; he was defiant and edgy, seemingly more scared of disappointing Shawn's mother than of being condemned by God. If Shawn had caught his mother sinning, he would've lectured her on right and wrong and God's plan for her life, but his father's a stern man, a Promise Keeper; challenging him leads to extra chores, raking the lawn again even though there aren't any leaves left, washing the car with a toothbrush. At bedtime, Shawn prayed for the strength to calm down, but this morning he was even more upset. He tiptoed into his parents' room while his father was in the shower and his mother was making breakfast and dug around for his father's cigarettes. They were in the sock drawer, barely even hidden—a soft new green pack, only two smoked. Shawn took them out one at a time and destroyed them. Then, regret and panic burning on his skin, he shoved as much of the evidence as possible back through the hole at the top of the wrapper and returned it to its hiding place. Sweeping the loose tobacco into his hand, Shawn ran to the half-bath by the laundry room, where, as his father yelped at the suddenly ice-cold water, he flushed it down the toilet.

The worst of it, though, was that next to the cigarettes in the drawer Shawn found a box of condoms. He knew what they were, but never having seen one up close, he stole a packet for future examination. He's been asking God for forgiveness all day, two, three, four times an hour and he plans to confess as soon as he can and be punished and start over, but what good will it do? He'll never be an extra-good Christian. The evil is creeping around in his body.

He sits in the new chair now, gazing out the picture window. He does this every Wednesday because his mother's not there to tell him the chair's too expensive and guests-only for him to crud up and also because there's some power in the sky, something invisible, something directly connected to his fear. The ritual does nothing to calm him down, but he is compelled to go through with it anyway, to watch the sun disappear and the streaky red and purple clouds change shape and hue, all the while monitoring the movements of his stomach muscles. They contract, squeezing out his goodness just like the sky does the sun.

The poplars and the cars, even the contents of the living room—his own skin—lose their color. The world goes black and white, a million shades of gray. He doesn't turn the light on. To do so would mean to move and he must remain very still. Something might see him and catch him if he moves. He won't even scratch his cheek; when it itches, he grimaces, clenches his eyes shut, works his mouth like he's chewing cud, anything to keep his hands frozen beneath his thighs.

Then, when he can't stand it one second longer he jumps up, his arms outstretched, ready to flail. Light from the streetlamp in front of the house slices a jagged triangle into the room; it ghosts at the edges and quivers as if it's afraid. He peers at the fire poker, the cd rack, the plants on their stands, the little things that move in the dark, slight vibrations when he stares straight at them, but when he's not looking, huge jerky shifts in the corner of his eye that halt abruptly as he tries to catch them.

Did God send the word down to Hell, "Hey, Satan, you know Shawn? Shawn Casper? He's done it again, and I'm getting fed up. This time he not only sat in the chair, he vandalized his father's cigarettes and stole a condom. He's a bad boy. He knows it. There's no excuse. Do you want him? He's kind of bony, but once you've got him, you can give him Gluttony, butter him up. He'll be nice and juicy in no time." Shawn dashes from room to room, pounding buttons and flicking switches. He taps the two lamps in the living room one, two, three times each, to their brightest brilliance. Even the bare bulbs in the basement have to be burning. He jumps, sometimes over and over, for the cords.

The whole house ablaze, he loops back to the bathroom and begins washing himself. The water steams as he thrusts his hands in. Whimpering, he holds them there until his skin goes numb. He scrubs with the antiseptic soft soap, with the lava soap, with the pumice stone his father uses on his feet. He rummages under the sink until he finds the can of petroleum hand gunk, scoops up half of it, and twists each finger until the joints ache. When the hot water begins to run out, he pumps some more soft soap into his palms and washes away the germs from the other soaps. He studies his face in the mirror and wishes he could see a good boy there.

He rushes to the kitchen and knocks the scrubbing powders and spray bottles and sponges and boxes of soap-caked steel wool under the sink around in search of cleaning supplies. He clutches the Windex and, banging his head on the plumbing, spins out of the cupboard. Yanking, he pulls three, four, five yards of paper towel off the roll. He runs to the new chair and touches it for the absolute last time, then he wipes all his previous touches away.

If only he could burn the book the minions tempt him with, but it's the Bible, and even if his intentions are good, it's the word of God. God wrote it. Better to continue cleaning, clean away all the oily fingerprints of the bad boy he's been up to now. He'll start where he is, wash the windows, the end tables, the lamps—that's tricky because when he touches them, they turn off. He has to dart in, pat, retreat, pat, retreat, pat, and there's light again. Find the next target and hit it three times. Daubing in inches until the whole lamp has been wiped clean. Every cd case and every cd, the TV set, the stereo, the whole entertainment center, even the *TV Guides* wedged in the cracks. He pulls the cushions off the couch and scoops out the rotting mints and cat-food crumbs and the lost Yahtzee dice, the paper clips and plastic half-inch guns. He cleans all four remote controls and the coffee table his father made during the year he tried carpentry. On to the fireplace. He cleans the poker, the prongs, the shovel. He cleans the rack that holds them. He scrubs the stone lip that juts out from the hearth. He scrubs the six logs waiting nearby for the night when they'll be ignited. The hearth itself, with its four inches of soot and its iron bars caked in spongy black gunk, with its dark chimney chute and the sharp tin sheet that bangs when you close it, is too scary to touch. What a great place for the minions to hide. He skips it, moves on to the mantel.

The crèche and the Jesse Tree have been replaced by a photo of the family, casually dressed but posed stiffly, and a decorative box his mother bought last year at Kmart. The one thing that stays all year long is the cross Shawn made out of burned wooden matches a few years ago, back when goodness came easy, in Sunday school. As he sprays and washes the cross, the matches begin to fall out like hair; the whole stupid thing breaks apart in his hands. While he cleans the photo, Windex creeps under the glass and attacks his family. He has better luck with the wooden box, scrubbing its inlaid surface and picking at the gunk lodged between the tiles—he has better luck, that is, until he opens it.

Inside the box, Shawn finds a zip-lock bag, and inside the bag is an inch-deep layer of crushed, dried leaves—at first Shawn thinks it's oregano, but it's clumpier, with seeds and stalks—and an unlabeled bottle with a dropper cap. Squeezing some liquid into the dropper, he notes its brown color, its sickly sweet smell, like molasses or medicine. Drugs.

Please, Jesus, please, please, make something bad happen to Mom and Dad so I can be orphaned and sent somewhere else. And make the place you send me be a good place with good Christian role models. Or at least just please, take me far away from the bad things here. What did I do, Jesus, that made You do this? Why did You make me have drug-addict parents? Please, Jesus, talk to me just once, just please. Then You never have to talk to me ever again. Cause I'm really a good boy, Jesus, and I tried to get born again and I tried to do

*everything You want me to and it's not my fault that Mom and Dad
are like they are. How come You won't ever talk to me and comfort me
like the Bible says You will? I want to talk to You more than anybody
has ever wanted to talk to You in the history of the world. Just this one
time, please, will You do what I ask You to? Please? Please, Please,
Please?*

Splayed on the floor, the drugs spread out in front of him,
Shawn bawls. His thoughts coalesce into this single word—
Please—repeated and ceaselessly repeated. No response booms
from on high, and as the seconds tumble and slow into minutes, as
the minutes stagnate and Shawn wallows in them, lukewarm and
numb, his mind wanders. Silence—*Please*—that's what God is.
God is—*Please*—this lack at the center of things. The nothing
that—*Please*—defines everything else as real. *Please . . . Please . . .
Please.* The thought that he will wait forever without hearing one
word from Jesus flits through Shawn's mind; it squirms away before
he understands it, replaced by an empty awareness of himself, sitting cross-legged on the floor, then lying flat on his stomach, alone.
But being alone is as meaningless to him as everything else now.
He no longer cries. The ringing in his ears is self-created and it's the
only thing that breaks the silence.

The strain and clank of the garage door wakes Shawn from
light sleep. He blinks at the carpet. It takes too much effort to
move, and for what? The commotion of his parents in the kitchen
bores him.

His father's voice shoots down the hallway, "Shawn? Shawn,
what are you doing with all the lights on?"

Shawn doesn't move. He thinks about how still he's lying.

"I've told you before, Shawn—only in the room you're plan-
ning on being in."

It seems like the living room is full of water, like his emotions
are floating somewhere on the surface while he lies here on the
floor, separated from the impetus to care about reprimands, lights,

his parents, Jesus Himself, by the dense mass of liquid that is pressing down on him. His body is alive, tingling with low-grade panic, but he is dead inside it.

Room by room, the house is going dark and his parents are coming toward him. Their presence in the room sucks the water from it. He feels claustrophobic. The panic moves through his bloodstream more quickly now, without the water weight to slow it down. Holding back tears asphyxiates him; it's like there's a balloon inflating in his throat.

His mother clicks out the seconds with her tongue. She steps over him and he can feel the air shift as she sweeps past and swoops down, picking things up off the floor.

His father sits on the edge of the couch, his knees wide; he leans low between them, his face bulging in toward Shawn's head. "Come on, Shawn. Let's sit up now."

With an abrupt, clumsy motion, almost like a rag doll, Shawn flops his head away. He sees his mother—her hands anyway—hiding the baggie and vial back in the box.

"Shawn, sit up and talk to us," his father says. "You're not a nine-year-old anymore."

He waits long enough to feel like it's his choice before doing what he's told. His every slight movement reverberates like sound through the shell of a bass drum. He scoots away, cradles his knees, and picks a point at which he can't see his parents to glare at.

"So, now, what's going on?" his father asks.

He promises himself not to say a word. He'll let his insolence speak for him, and when they ask questions, his silence will be close to that of God.

"Look at this place, Shawn. It's—the lights are on, there are cleaning products strewn all over the kitchen, there's greasy stuff all over the bathroom sink—"

"Hand goop," Shawn says before he can stop himself.

"—And look at this, Shawn, you destroyed your cross. I'm thinking, what's going on?" His father's face goes slack, waiting for an answer. "Shawn?" His head wobbles back and forth. "I can't even—Shawn, what happened here?"

"I . . ."

His father studies a cluster of matches. "I can't hear you, Shawn."

Shawn slumps his shoulders. He shrugs.

"Is this the game we're playing? You think if you don't say anything then everything will be okay? You going to wait us out and maybe it'll go away?"

"Chad, it's just a little matchstick cross."

This is wrong, too, to let her defend him.

"I'm not angry. I'm not—look, we're having a conversation. About responsibility and grown-up things like that. It's not like I'm going to . . . we're just talking. Right, Shawn?"

Shawn combusts. His body is on fire. The water has fled and he's grown dry and brittle. Now he's in flames, his every cell bursting. His skin cracks and crackles. His sinews shrink in the heat. He speaks and it's as if the words are all one long syllable popping out in a sparkle of red coal.

"I didn't do it on purpose I was trying to make it clean and it broke and it doesn't matter cause I don't care cause it doesn't matter." The words catch and tangle on top of each other; for a moment, they squeeze into gibberish, guttural sounds that feel like they're springing from Shawn's pores, not his mouth. "It's cause you're drug addicts."

"What?"

"Don't pretend."

"Shawn, what? We're *drug* addicts?"

"What's that, then? That's drugs. You're drug addicts."

"Shawn, we're . . . this is catnip."

"See? You're lying now. I knew you were going to lie, cause you're liars and drug addicts and liars and you're bad. You're just bad and you made me bad, too." He's gutted now. Everything has been burned out.

"It's catnip. Look. You put it in the little mouse and the cat plays with it."

"Then what about the bottle? That's not catnip. What about that, then?"

"That's for his worms."

"Izzy doesn't have worms."

"Not anymore, because this stuff got rid of them. Look at it . . . See? Don't you remember? We had to hold his mouth open and take the dropper and push the medicine down his throat." Shawn's mother holds the bottle up for his inspection, but he turns his head away. He won't be lied to.

"Okay, Shawn? Is that all that's wrong?"

Is that all that's wrong.

"Well, then, how come . . . then, how come it's all hidden like drugs?"

"It's just hidden from the cat."

"But, then . . . then . . ." Suddenly, exhausted, he falls onto his back and covers his eyes. Tension spikes through his jaw, into his chest. Behind his eyelids, splotches of color flicker and ghost and then disappear. His pulse pounds in his neck. They're lying and he knows it. Otherwise, Jesus would talk to him—no, that's not true, he knows better than that. The truth is that his mother's telling the truth, and this disturbs Shawn more than anything—to have gone through all he's gone through tonight and discover it was for naught. His faith has left him and in its place there's just wind.

Without looking, he feels his parents lingering. Its like he's a sensor and they're infrared; heat patterns on either side of him. Or sentries from someone else's religion, guarding his cold body against the night. They make no noise as they shift on their haunches. He surmises that they're communicating with each other in a parent language made up of hand signs and grimaces. One of them places a thumb to his forehead; the lightness of touch, the tenderness with which the thumb trails toward his brow before it's whisked away, tells him it's his mother. He wants to reach up and be held by her, but now they're gone from the room and the air chills behind them.

Later, when he opens his eyes, the house is dark.

Shawn catches himself asking, *Jesus, please help me get a good grade* as he sits at his school desk behind a math test. He shudders and stops himself. What's the use?

At recess he stands on the edge of the soccer field, watching his classmates play French tag. His arms are crossed and his face is stern. He's not condemning them, though that's what it looks like. He is condemning himself for his urge to condemn them. They run in circles like chickens, tackling each other, kissing and groping and kissing. He can no longer say with conviction that what they're doing is wrong—Jesus is no longer on his side. Maybe He never was. He feels like a very old man, and his classmates are far away from him. They are children, innocents, somehow able to act without thinking, to run and tackle and kiss and grope without worrying about the meaning of their actions. Shawn imagines that as opposed to him—who pours his every urge through a moral filter, and then does nothing for fear of doing something wrong—they live on impulse, with immediacy, and are able to interpret what happens to them through ad hoc, ever-changing conceptions of their connection to the life around them. He's in a gray zone between what he believed just last week and an alternative he can't conceive of. He wishes he could join the other kids and play, simply play. He surveys the girls chasing around the field. They're mostly flat-chested and lanky, distinguishable from the boys only by haircut. One girl attracts his attention, though. Her thin brown hair blows like flax in the wind; her vineyards are, if not in bloom, at least budding; her fawns nuzzle their heads against her sweater. Unlike most of the other girls, she isn't chasing a specific boy. Instead, she kicks around the field halfheartedly, awkward and shy as she loops through the throng. Shawn could catch her easily.

She's a grade above him, and he doesn't even know her name. If he caught her, he could pull her to the ground like the other boys do and lie on top of her. He could clamp her wrists above her head and then he could kiss her and then he could, he's not sure, maybe say something that would make her smile so she wanted to kiss him too. Even though he's pretty sure that God wouldn't crack lightning down on his head for this—God isn't listening, God isn't looking—Shawn can't bring himself to act. For one thing, he'd get dirty rolling around in the grass, stains on his jeans and his white oxford shirt, scuffs on his shoes, his hair all affray. For another, just because God doesn't care, because God isn't there, does that mean it's okay to tackle the girl? She might cry and pull his hair. She might be angry with him. She might bite his tongue off. Shawn wanders away from the soccer field and contemplates the four-square court painted on the pavement in front of the school, hoping his thing relaxes before he's called in from recess.

When he gets home, Shawn sits in the new chair and stares out the window, spinning his finger in figure eights across his left temple. He leaves his post for dinner only at his father's command. He cleans his plate quickly, mumbles "Can I be excused?" and then leaps back into his plastic-wrapped throne. He's looking for something out there in the night, but he doesn't know what it is. There's no word for it. He doesn't bother to ask God for insight. Instead he derides himself: he is too timid, he hides behind faith, when, really, why shouldn't he have chased down the girl on the soccer field and kissed her? There are so many things he's turned away from for fear of where he'd end up if he walked toward them. Why shouldn't he have looked at the *Playboy* the tough boys in the bathroom tried to force on him before they gave him a swirly? Really, what's so wrong with rock-and-roll music that he should deny himself its pumping beat? Why shouldn't he do whatever he wants? Why not? There are no reprisals. There's just him gazing out at the phone lines and streetlights, the brown matted grass, the houses and houses that look just like his.

That night, Shawn tempts himself to break taboos, to somehow become a normal boy like the ones chasing girls on the soccer field. He searches the family bookshelves for anything that might contain a dirty part, and finding nothing, imagines the girl with flaxen hair stepping into his room on her tiptoes. He knows now that there are no minions; there is only himself. Shawn no longer resists. He lets himself be overcome with impure thoughts and onanizes late into the night. The sex clenches his body, but as it does, his impure thoughts gallop around in his mind. They don't take control of him, though, not this time. Now he's in control of them, spurring them on, until he's just body with no mind at all, eighty-eight pounds of sensation. Proudly, triumphantly, he makes the stain. It looks and tastes like snot.

There's no reason to feel guilty, but he does anyway. He's not sure what to do with this feeling. Guilt is just another something caught in space with him. He has no hierarchy in which to place himself, no gameboard on which to move two spaces ahead or be penalized back to Start; he no longer even understands the objective of the game. There is no reason for anything. Good or bad, right or wrong, none of it really matters. Wherever he goes, whatever he does, this thought keeps rolling back into his head: what does it matter? It doesn't. He's at Wal-Mart coveting a cd, and what if he stole it? It wouldn't matter. The only reason he doesn't slip the cd under his shirt is that if he's caught he'll get thrown in jail. He plays with the condom he took from his dad, rips open the package, unrolls the rubber, tries it on, takes it off, blows it up to watch it fly around his bedroom. He wonders how many hundreds of millions of condoms the condom company makes every year. An entire industry exists solely to sheath people's things, what's wrong with that? Nothing, that's what. He stops folding his clothes. He parts his hair differently, and sometimes, he doesn't part it at all. He wears dirty underwear now sometimes, and more and more often he doesn't bother to wash his hands after he pees. What does it matter? Nothing matters.

The night before Easter, he stays up late and, after his parents have gone to bed, he slinks into the living room, turns the TV on mute and scans the stations. Showtime and Cinemax are the forbidden fruit he has on his mind tonight. The kids at school who know this kind of thing believe Cinemax is better—Skinemax they call it. He gives it a try. His family doesn't subscribe, so it's scrambled, but that doesn't stop him from watching. A greenish-gray bar divides the screen horizontally and a pulsing line of colors divides it vertically, cutting the picture into four pieces, each in the wrong place, like one of those plastic slide puzzles. The image flips and squiggles, but every few seconds it catches and he can make out what he's watching. Three hands, one red, one green, one blue, mirror each other in a sliding motion over a smooth surface. As the fingers massage this surface, sharp white lines streak behind them like barbs. The picture cuts to a different shot and Shawn sees two green nipples on a blue breast. A man with green lips leans in to kiss them and suddenly there's only one nipple. The picture breaks up into jerky spasms, then goes back to the flips and squiggles. If he concentrates, Shawn can slow the images down. The parts that are scrambled can be inferred. A man with blue hair is having sex with a woman with green hair. Their lips are white and float free from their bodies. Shawn touches his thing and stares at the screen. He doesn't go to bed until three-thirty a.m.

His parents drag him out of the house before dawn, and he sleeps in the family Festiva as they drive through the fog to the sunrise service. Folding chairs have been assembled in a semicircle around the damp knoll east of church, and Shawn's family, late because he wouldn't get up, is stuck in a row near the back. He shivers in the early-morning chill and does all he can to stay awake. He fidgets with his program. He frowns through the hymns. During the sermon, he slides off his chair and squirms, plucking blades of grass and tying them in knots. His father casts a look. His mother pats the chair. He climbs off his knees and sits limp, his head swaying back and forth, jolting sometimes when it feels like it's going to fall off. He draws Easter eggs on his program. He paints his finger-nails with the highlighter he finds in his mother's purse. He doesn't hear a word Preacher Dan says.

At communion, he shuffles up to the front of the line, eats his pellet of baked dough and downs his shot of grape juice. He feels like a huckster, tricking the people into thinking he's with them in fellowship when, in truth, he's merely going through the motions, as empty of passion as this ritual is of meaning. The dough is stale, the juice watered down. He misses the sense of purpose, the soaring project, the urgency that blind faith once allowed him. He wipes his lips with the back of his hand.

As the service ends, Preacher Dan faces the congregation from the top of the hill. He has shaved off his mustache, and without it, the skin around his scar seems puffier. Over his suit he wears a thin white robe, ruffled at the neck and boxy, with no arms, just slits for his hands, which rise now above him, palms out toward Heaven. The robe billows like wings from his wrists to his knees. High wisps of cloud hover pink and gold above him, a sky right out of an uplifting poster. A sliver of sun breaks over the hill and Preacher Dan's voice booms out across the congregation, "This is the day that the Lord has made."

It's met with exuberance. "Let us rejoice and be glad in it."

Shawn is woozy with exhaustion. He grips the chair in front of him to keep from collapsing. He's so tired he twitches. Preacher Dan seems to be sitting on top of the sun, his legs dangling toward the ground, and Shawn, in his exhaustion, almost believes this is more than an illusion, that Dan really is floating, and not just floating—ascending. Shawn doesn't want to burn his retinas. He bows his head and blinks the light away.

"Hallelujah, Christ is risen."

Everyone but Shawn raises their hands above their heads.

Words Shawn has known his whole life tap through his mind. *For God so loved the world, that He gave His only begotten Son, that whosoever believes in Him should not perish, but have everlasting life, forever and ever, A-men.* They have such a seductive, treacherous lilt. He thinks about what he was up to last night and wonders if it shows on his face.

Every voice but Shawn's soars and swoops, "The Lord is risen indeed, Hallelujah."

The sun is free of the Earth now. Preacher Dan stands inside it, his body a silhouette, the robe outstretched, diaphanous, filtering the rays. Warmth tugs at Shawn's eyelids; he could fall asleep where he's standing. The morning light makes everything crisp— undeniably real. The texture of the plastic chair back in Shawn's hands, the bright prints and pastels of his fellow parishioners' Easter clothes, the dew on the grass on the hill leading to Preacher Dan, all these things are so convincingly what they are. Compared to this world, Shawn feels abstract, vague and hazy, like a scribble that could mean anything.

He shouts—"The Lord is risen indeed, Hallelujah"—but the rest of the voices have already faded. His cracking soprano flails like an out-of-tune trumpet, alone, announcing how profoundly he's failed the Lord.

Preacher Dan is a dark spot on the sun, his face eclipsed by the brilliance behind him. His voice floats to Earth across light-years. "That boy's going to make a great preacher one day."

The congregation sighs. Shawn's father bows his head. His mother scruffs up his hair.

Jesus, is that You? Does this mean I'm saved?

The heat graces Shawn's skin.

McNeil, Layla

u32.3691341

She'll be ten years old the first time. She won't even notice it's happened—or she'll almost not notice. She'll know something's not right the way she knows smog's diseased sky: by the sick feeling she has about it later. But she won't comprehend what has changed in her life. Because they'll be an intimate family, prone to backrubs and cuddles and nibbles on the ear, because personal space will be something they share and this sharing will symbolize love and filial devotion, because she'll be taught to trust in her father, that nothing can hurt her, there's nothing to fear if her father is within arm's reach, and his adoring eyes will assure her it's true and she will believe him and wrap her arms tighter around his neck and burrow her face deeper into his shoulder, for all these reasons, she'll let him kiss her belly and blow foghorn farts that will rumble throughout her whole body; he'll get her to laugh and squeal, to quiver in her skin like waiting for Christmas with all its surprise and presents and change. When he lets his finger slip into her, she won't know it's wrong: a thin little membrane is all that exists between Daddy protect me and Daddy don't hurt me and she'll be too young to have known it was there to be broken. No, the way she will learn is through absence: the pulling away and the public slights and the rigid spike in his muscles when she wraps her arms tighter around his neck. His fear, like an index of what's in the air, will clue her in to what she's become. A sunset through smog is more vibrant, smeared with a far broader range of colors, than sunsets naturally are. She'll dwell in her smog-imbued sunset for forty-odd years before she follows it finally into the dark.

MERIT BADGE

I don't know who started the lie that Boy Scouts is a club for fags and puds, but whoever it was'll be sorry if he's ever lost in the woods without one of us around. A Boy Scout would be able to tell him what berries are poisonous and what ones you can eat and he'd know how to build a rabbit trap out of twigs laying on the ground, and even if nobody had any matches, he'd still be able to get a fire lit to cook that rabbit. A Scout would have all kinds of nature know-how so everybody could find their way back to town without getting killed by a bear and stuff. If he didn't have a Scout around, that guy who thinks he's too-cool wouldn't even be able to figure out which way is north and he'd probably starve or die of frostbite or something and nobody would ever find him until all his muscles had gotten eaten by wolves and the rest of him was all disintegrated.

So I could learn stuff like that and go camping and stuff is why I joined Boy Scouts. I didn't join so I could run around naked in the woods with other boys. That would be like going out for football so you could take showers with the football players, and nobody would do that. If you even thought about getting a woody in the shower with everybody there and everything, you'd get beat up.

That's why it's not fair I'm getting kicked out now . . .

o   o   o

One of the other cool things Scouts do is me and Jake and the rest of the troop built a lookout tower in the high school gym up in Oshkosh at the Boy Scout Expo. And yesterday we got to build one again at the Jamboree. We didn't kill any trees or anything cause we were careful and found a whole bunch of really long dead ones that we could make into these great big poles and we scraped the bark off so they were all white and shiny and stuff. Then we took other trees and cut them up to tie up in squares that sort of got smaller and smaller the higher you climbed on the tower. And we made floors on every square so it could be three floors tall. And we made railings so you can't fall off. And a ladder too, so you could get up there. It was like sixty feet big, and it was way cooler than the one in the Boy Scout manual.

After we made the Expo one, Jake climbed all the way to the top before anybody else could even get there and then he shouted, "I'm king of the lookout tower, hear me roar!" and then he roared and it was really loud all over the gym and everybody shut up and looked at him, so he walked around and roared some more and stuff, and then he raised his arms like a World Wrestling champion except his gold belt was pretend. Mr. Schultz was getting all mad and walking back and forth and stuff, so Jake grabbed on to the metal beam things on the roof of the gym and swung on them like he was gonna do the monkey bars all the way across to the bleachers. After that, Mr. Schultz climbed up and made Jake get down right now so we could do rope making and knot tying like we were supposed to. When Jake was back off the tower, everybody told him how cool he was and everything, and he got even tougher, like even more cool.

For like three hours at the Expo I had to tie knots on the second floor. It got so boring cause I only know about five knots and I had to do them over and over again and none of the people who were supposed to look at us tying knots were looking at us anyway. There were like a hundred and fifty troops in the gym all doing different things, and except for our tower, what we were doing was the most boring of any of them—everybody already knows how to tie knots. There was this one thing that looked cool that I wanted to go see, this troop had this big glass jar with all kinds of chemicals and stuff in it and they had this thing that spun around and pulled string out of the chemicals even though there wasn't any string in them. I wanted to go look at that, but we weren't allowed to cause we had to just tie knots all day.

After I got bored, I made a noose though. I took this like thirty-foot-long rope and tied a great big huge noose on one end and I made the other end into a pile so I could hold it on the other side of the railing. Then I put the noose around my waist really tight, and held on to the rope and jumped off the edge of the tower. It was so cool cause I could pull myself up and down with the other part of the rope and everybody was watching me and stuff. But when Mr. Schultz saw, he started screaming at me that I was gonna break my neck—pretty stupid, cause the noose was around my waist and even if I fell, I wasn't very high up or anything. He made me get down and not go on the tower again for the rest of the day cause it was such a baby thing to do what I did. Like I'm a Webelos or something. Jake gave me a high five, though, and then I got to go look at that spinny thing with the chemicals, so that was good. The people explained that the chemicals mix up with each other and when they touch the air they turn into nylon, like morphing or something. Pretty trippy.

Anyway, it wasn't a big deal or anything. Even though I did the thing with the noose, the Expo gave our tower first prize. That's why we got to build one in the middle of Elkhart Lake for the Jamboree . . .

When Jake went camping before, there was this bunch of high school kids in the spot next to his mom and dad's camper and they had this watermelon that they'd cut a hole in and poured in like a ton of vodka so it got all mixed up with the watermelon. If you do that, you get drunker without even tasting it. Jake partied with them every day and one night, he even got to put his hand down this one girl's underpants and feel around in there and he stuck his finger in her thing. He let me smell the finger, but I couldn't smell anything except cigarettes cause Jake smokes and stuff with Chewy. And the girl let him do that to her even though she's like a senior and a cheerleader up in Oconomowoc. She's got really big boobs and she's like in love with him and everything now.

Once, I asked Jake if I could meet her and he said maybe, but I know he's not gonna let me. Every time I say anything, he tells me all the things I can't do in front of her. I can't talk about Boy Scouts. I can't talk about comic books or Jim Carrey movies. I can't even talk about *The X-Files*. And that's basically everything there is to talk about. Anyway, Jake's even more into *The X-Files* than me, I didn't even watch it until he explained to me how deep it was about all the important stuff people should think about. And his comic book collection's like fifty times bigger than mine. And he knows every line of *The Mask* by heart.

He won't even tell me her name cause it'll jinx it. Every time I ask him about her, he gets all nervous and mad and stuff and starts shaking his leg really hard.

What it is I bet is that Chewy told him *The X-Files* and comic books and Jim Carrey movies and stuff were faggy and that his girl-friend would break up with him if he was into them. I bet Chewy told Jake I'm faggy too cause I'm into that stuff. Or else I bet Jake's girlfriend's fake.

If I wanted to I could come up with a better fake girlfriend than Jake and maybe even a real girlfriend. But if I got a real girlfriend I wouldn't tell Jake about it or anything cause that would be private . . .

○   ○   ○

I'm not a fag. And I'm not a pud, neither. Fag and pud is like what everybody says about people in Boy Scouts, so Jake and Chewy should think about that before they start saying stuff like that. They should think about that and not be so much like people who aren't Scouts. Otherwise it's all two-faced and everything.

I could stop being a Scout if I wanted but then I wouldn't know what to be. And if I did that I couldn't do all the cool stuff we do. And Jake and Chewy and everybody would all say I stopped cause they don't like me and walk around at meetings saying stuff about how I'm a fag cause remember when I did whatever and I wouldn't even get to say they were liars.

Anyway, I got four merit badges already. I got the Swimming. I got the Fire Safety. I got the Knots. I got the First Aid. And one day when I'm an Eagle Scout, I'll have more . . .

Elkhart Lake's cool. Except for the racetrack and the parking lot and the snack bar and the humungous shower place that smells so much like people went to the bathroom in it you can't breathe, it's all like woods and stuff with a whole bunch of trees in these really straight rows that people planted a long time ago after they chopped all the old ones down. The lake isn't a real lake, though. Somebody made it. But it's still way cool, with like fish and logs and stuff floating in it just like a real one has. Mr. Schultz says there's deer and possums and raccoons in the woods, but I don't believe him. I haven't seen any, anyway.

The best thing at Elkhart Lake is that it's got girls that live on the other side where there's houses and it's not a Boy Scout Jamboree place with a racetrack and everything. They go out waterskiing and stuff and they're really pretty too.

When me and Jake went canoeing in the lake, there was this motorboat full of girls getting tans and laying on the front of the boat and stuff, and they had their tops undone, so I said, "Let's row over closer to them, then maybe they'll sit up and forget their tops are undone and maybe we'll get to see their boobs." But Jake said, "No, I can look at boobs anytime I want on my girlfriend."

"Not this week," I said.

"But any other time."

"Don't you want to see other boobs, too, though?" I said and he looked at me all mean like I was the one being weird so I said, "And those girls are like really good-looking."

"So what," he said.

"So we should go try to see their boobs."

"That would make my girlfriend jealous."

"But don't you *want* to see their boobs?"

"Will you stop fucking whining?" he said.

"You don't have to shout!" I shouted and he splashed his paddle and sprayed water all over me, and then there was this girl's voice that sounded fake sweet but really mean like a cheerleader or something and she said, "Hey, are you guys *Boy Scouts?*"

"No," said Jake.

The girls were so close now you could see their faces even, and they were all looking at us. This one girl was sitting up but she didn't have her top off anymore. The other two did, though, and I wanted to stand up cause their boobs were sort of laying there, all round and almost not pressed down on the boat anymore. I bet I could've seen them too, but it would've been really obvious of me.

"We're building a lookout tower," I said and Jake gave me a dirty look and everybody sat there feeling weird and stuff.

"So, are you guys like afraid of girls or something?" said the girl without her top undone.

"No," said Jake.

"You seem like it."

"We're not scared of girls. Jake's got a girlfriend even," I said and then he whispered "Shut up" really loud.

"Lucky girl," she said, and Jake's face got all red and then he said, "Hey, listen, I'm not trying to be rude or nothing, but we got stuff to do. We can't sit around talking to you all afternoon."

The girl laughed like tee-hee and said, "How old are you?"

"Sixteen," he said and looked at me like I better not say he's lying. As if that's something I'd do anyway.

"And I'm fifteen and a half," I said and all the girls laughed so I laughed too, but Jake gave me another dirty look.

"So, see ya," Jake said and then he started rowing, but one of the girls reached around to tie her top back on and sat up really fast and put her fingers under it to make it go on right and I'm almost sure I saw her boobs for a second, so I didn't help him. "Don't be a fag, Evan, help me row," he said, and I had to cause otherwise it would've looked bad in front of the girls.

I turned around and waved while we rowed away and the girl whose boobs I saw said, "Hey, are you guys here all week?" Even though she was talking to me, Jake said, "Yeah," and she said, "We're out here every day. Maybe we'll see you later," and Jake shrugged and said, "That's cool."

Then the girls pulled the chain on their motor and speeded away.

Me and Jake rowed over to where there was a hidden part with trees and bushes and stuff growing right in the water. I wanted to tell him that he shouldn't be mad at me cause he's the one who didn't want to talk to them and then got all too-cool when they came over. And he didn't have to call me a fag and stuff right in front of them. So after I couldn't hold it any longer I said, "You don't have to make fun of me in front of girls, Jake," and he said, "Well, maybe if you didn't act so stupid all the time, I wouldn't," like he was better than me or something.

He stopped rowing and started smoking a cigarette, and then he laid down on the end of the canoe and smiled at me, but it wasn't a nice smile, and he was making these really big smoke rings. I could tell he was waiting for me to say something else that he could be mean about, so I said, "I don't know why you care anyway. You've got a girlfriend."

"I *don't* care," he said.

"Yeah, right. Then why'd you pretend to be sixteen and stuff?"

"No reason. Just to have fun."

"I bet you don't even *have* a girlfriend." I never even thought that before I said it, but then it seemed like it was true cause he got all nervous and he sat up and stopped being too-cool and everything.

"Jealous?" he said.

"No."

He made this I-don't-believe-you sound, so I said, "Then how come you won't tell me her name, then, huh?"

"You know what, Chewy's right. You *are* a pud."

"No, I'm not."

"I mean, you're such a fag. You're such a dick-whacker. You wouldn't know what to do with a girl if you had one."

"Yes I would."

"I bet. What would you do?"

I didn't know what to say for a second and then it started to be too long, so I said, "What would *you* do?"

"I asked you first."

"I'd, I don't know, talk to her and stuff."

"Fag."

"And . . . and I'd like look at her boobs and play with them."

Jake was smiling like he was making fun of me and I was almost crying cause it seemed like he didn't even like me anymore.

"And I'd play with her thing."

"You're such a fag, Evan! Girls don't have things!" He laughed and laughed and laughed like he was almost gonna fall out of the canoe and I couldn't think of anything else to say, so I said, "What's her name?" and Jake laughed at me some more. "What's her name? If you don't tell me her name, she must not be real," I said and Jake scrunched up his face and said, "What's her name what's her name what's her name?" in this extra whiny, squeaky voice. And then he like pouted and put his fingers together to do the world's tiniest violin thing I hate.

I held my stomach really tight and my eyes were all like they were burning and I yelled, "Tell me her name, you fucker! Why won't you tell me her name?" and I rocked the canoe back and forth as hard as I could so the sides almost touched the water and Jake started crawling over the seats and stuff so he could get up by me and he said, "You wanna fight, fag? Is that what you want? I'll beat you up if that's what you want so bad." So I rocked even harder than I thought I could until he fell in the water and the canoe tipped over and I fell in too.

I hid in the upside-down part where it's like an air space cause then if Jake wanted to say sorry or whatever he couldn't just do it like he didn't mean it, like everything was all cool and stuff. The water was echo-y and extra loud under the canoe so I couldn't hear anything outside and there were like white glowing lines from the water reflecting all over the metal. It wasn't really dark or anything so I held the wood things and waited for him to come say sorry. He didn't even have a choice, cause he couldn't swim that far back to camp and I wasn't gonna let the canoe get turned upside up until he did.

He didn't for a long time, but that was okay cause there was lots of air in my air space. I started to get scared, though, like maybe he drowned or got twisted up in the lily pads and hit his head on a dead log or something, so I put my head underwater and opened my eyes just to see if you could see down there. I wished Jake would come and say sorry soon and then I'd never talk about his stupid girlfriend again even if she was fake cause then at least he wouldn't be dead. Floaty things kept swimming between my legs and I was getting really really scared. Well, not really, but sort of, cause I didn't know what happened to Jake.

Then the canoe started shaking really fast and bouncing around and I spazzed out and screamed really loud and then Jake came up inside the canoe and spit a big wad of water at me. He was grinning, though, and I laughed, I was so happy it was just him.

He said, "It's cool in here."

"Uh-huh."

And then it was like I wasn't mad at him anymore even though I still wanted to be. He shouldn't have been so mean to me, though, even if I was acting spazzy and stuff, cause I was just trying to figure stuff out about him and there was no reason for him to be mean. It seems like if he was my best friend like he always used to be he wouldn't make fun of me and try to make me mad and everything. I'm not a baby or a fag or a pud or any of the things he said I was, I just wanted him to keep being my best friend.

After that was the stupidest thing I did, but I thought he was being my friend again and I had to cause I didn't want him to really turn into like he didn't care and not be my best friend anymore just like that. And I was starting to think maybe it was my fault and stuff, so I did the stupid thing. I asked him how come if he didn't want to talk to those girls anyway, he had to be all mean to me to show them how cool he was.

"No reason," he said.

I couldn't stop trying to find out if he hated me, so I said, "Really? No reason?"

"It's never cool to be un-cool with girls," he said.

"But—"

"They were ugly anyway. Come on."

"Wait, though," I said but he swam out of the canoe. I stayed inside cause maybe he'd come back then but he didn't and I had to swim out too so I could keep talking to him.

"Evan, get on that end and—"

"Wait, though, Jake."

"No, you have to be farther than that, Evan, all the way at the end. It's lighter then."

"But Jake, wait."

"What?" and he sounded all mad again.

"Don't yell at me, Jake. I mean, just don't yell at me, okay? Please?"

He didn't say anything but he looked sort of less mad then.

"I . . ." I didn't want to say something wrong right away because then by the time I said something right he'd be mad at me again and he'd yell at me and never be my friend again, so I made up in my head what to say over and over again but Jake looked like he was going to be mad again anyway so I said, "Because I don't want you not to like me anymore, Jake. You're always acting like you don't like me and stuff now . . . Cause . . . Why don't you like me? Jake? How come?"

"Can't you just go to your side so we can turn the canoe over? Or do you want to get me on KP, too?"

"But can't you just tell me, Jake?"

"Don't be a . . ." I got like all crinkly cause he was gonna say pud or fag again, but he didn't, he said "girl" and I started to cry and I didn't have anything more to say then.

Both of us looked at each other for a long time and I got the sniffles trying to make myself stop crying. I didn't even think about anything except trying not to go underwater. My head was all like my brain was burning up and Jake wouldn't stop looking at me.

Then he said, "I didn't mean that, Evan," and I felt like I couldn't be a Boy Scout anymore.

It started getting really dark when we figured out how to turn the canoe upside up by pushing really hard and then when it fell back the other way sort of throwing it really fast. When I got in Jake had to let me step on him and I thought it was gonna turn over again but it didn't and I held it so Jake could get in too but he swam away.

"Where are you going?"

"Just relax. I'm going over here—I gotta take a shit."

"In the water?"

"Yup."

"But . . . you can do that?"

"Yup."

"But isn't that like bad and stuff?"

"Nope."

"But won't the fish eat it and get sick?"

"Nope."

That's why Jake was my best friend, cause he could do things that nobody told him were okay but he just knew. It was such a cool thing of Jake.

"It feels good too. Like free. You feel the water go all around your balls and you just let go and"— and he made like an "Ah" and an "Ooo" sound like his muscles were all tight and then when he was done, he smiled. "Like that," he said. "Heaven."

Then we rowed back to camp not talking or anything but not like we were mad at each other either . . .

Jake told me this story about this cool thing he did with Chewy one day. They went to the gas station and stole a porno magazine and a book of sexy letters from people who wrote to *Penthouse*. It was really cool except it was with Chewy and he doesn't like me. The way they did it was that Jake went in before Chewy and asked the guy if he could buy some cigarettes and when the guy said no he got all mad and started saying how not fair that was and everything and then the guy got all mad too and they started to fight and stuff so that when they were fighting Chewy could take the stuff without the guy seeing. And then Jake walked out all in a huff and Chewy bought a pack of Skittles and they went and looked at the magazines and Chewy even let Jake keep the *Penthouse* thingee. I saw it. I bet that's why Jake and Chewy are like best friends and everything now.

But what if Jake was friends with Chewy and with me too? If like me and Jake went camping and Chewy came with because Jake told him how cool I was even though I'm no good at sports and stuff. And then Chewy wouldn't be mean to me anymore and we could all be best friends and be Eagle Scouts together. That would be great.

Chewy's already a First Class Scout and everybody likes him.

He's called Chewy cause he got drunk with this girl at this party once. He just got sort of drunk but he got her so drunk she couldn't even stand up or anything. And then they like went into a room where there was nobody there and they kissed and played with each other's things and Chewy even got her to let him see her boobs and stuff. He didn't hit a home run though cause the other people were spying on them and they like opened the door really fast and turned on the lights and when they did that Chewy was chewing on the nipple part of her boob so it was all sore and stuff and then the girl barfed and everybody got mad at her cause she was gonna make them get caught having a party. And that's why Chewy's Chewy. If he wasn't so mean to me he would be really cool . . .

The other thing Elkhart Lake's got is a really great beach part where they have a float in the deep end that you can dive off and everything. They got a net thing that goes all around it to keep the fish out and all these red and white floaty things that tell the motorboats not to come in.

We get swim time every day for like an hour. That's the funnest part, cause then we can play king of the float.

You're not allowed to swim in the deep end except if you take a swim test with every different kind of stroke around the whole edge by the net, otherwise you have to stay in the baby part where it's only like up to your knees and there's no splashing or diving or nothing. The swim test's really hard cause everybody's watching and you can't stop or slow down or anything or else you fail. The good thing is you get to try again until you pass but I didn't have to. I passed on the first try even though I didn't think I could cause when I try to do the butterfly I just stay in one place and go around in a circle over and over again. They decided that was okay cause I did everything else really good. Chewy said they were just being nice to me cause they thought I was gonna cry, but he had to take the test like fifty times before they let him not swim in the baby part and he was just jealous. I wouldn't have cried anyway cause I'm not a crybaby.

Swimming in the deep end is really cool when there's a whole bunch of people and we can play king of the float and everything. Even though I'm sort of weak, I do pretty good sometimes cause I'm really writhey and slippery so it's really hard to catch me. That's what I'm good at is keeping everybody from throwing me off. I'm not so good at pushing people off cause when I do I fall off too, but I can stay up for a long time if I just keep writhing away. I even won before by staying up while everybody else pushed everybody else off until I was the only one left.

The funnest thing is to get thrown off so you go way up in the air before you come down. What you do is when you know you can't stay on any longer, you make yourself get really light and let one of the big guys throw you way up in the air. It's really cool cause then your stomach goes around and around like a roller coaster and it's like you're gonna stay up in the air for a really long time until you're underwater and you don't even know when you stopped being in the air and started being in the water, like the air just got thicker or something. It's really weird cause it's like everything's the same thing and the hard things and the soft things and the air and the water and even you and everything else are just pretend different. But it's not weird in a bad way, cause it's still sort of really cool.

Today I could barely stay on for two seconds. Chewy was king of the float and he figured out this way to push you off before you were even on, like you'd pull yourself up and Chewy would kick from way far away when you were still only half over and for like a long time nobody could un-king him.

It got to be no fun anymore so we stopped trying to get up. We just treaded water and acted all bored and then Chewy told us how he could whip our ass and how we were chicken and he made like squawky sounds and then he sat down in the middle of the float and told us we were the ones being boring. I bet he knew it was his fault but he had to act like it was all our fault anyway cause he won and got to be king and no way would he ever think he did something wrong cause it's winning that counts.

Then everybody got all together to try and figure out how to un-king Chewy so it would get fun again. We treaded water in like a football huddle and nobody could figure anything out till I said maybe if we all climbed up at the same time, like count to three or something, cause then there'd be too many of us and we could probably get up but first we should all be like we don't care and like we're not doing anything. Everybody thought that was a good idea and we went to get in our spots and I swam to the other side by going under the float and through the big chains and stuff tied to the bottom of the water and Chewy didn't know how I got there or anything and then we all treaded water in our places and looked at each other like who was gonna count to three.

Chewy was thinking he was so cool and everything that he didn't even see we were getting ready to un-king him till we were all halfway up the float already and stuff and then he looked scared till he said, "Hey, Jake, tag team!" and helped to pull Jake up so they could tag team against everybody and Chewy could win again and everything. Even though it made Jake a traitor he didn't even care.

I was the only one who could get up cause Chewy and Jake's tag team was good enough to throw everybody off. I got right in back of Chewy and made myself way low to the float so I could slide on my stomach and stuff and then I grabbed Chewy's foot and pulled really hard even though it got all twisty trying to make me let go. I tried to get his other foot too so I could have them both and like pull him off with both of them but he kept stepping really hard on my fingers so I couldn't. The good thing is, though, he couldn't kick the people climbing up, anymore, so our side started winning. And then instead of trying to get his other foot I twisted my body all around his legs and made it so he couldn't move and I started to like roll back and forth but he still wouldn't fall down so I just stayed like that so everybody else could get Jake off easier without Chewy helping and stuff. Then when that was done everybody started pushing Chewy but that was harder cause he's so big and he was even heavier with me on his feet so he sort of just moved a little closer to the edge every time and my back was getting all scraped up by the AstroTurf the float's made out of. We got right by the edge and then everybody pushed all at the same time and Chewy fell in the water but he pulled everybody else in at the same time and my back got even more scraped up cause when I tried to get off Chewy's leg he kicked me in the face.

Jake was king of the float then cause he climbed up when we were all falling in . . .

In the dictionary when I looked it up once, it said a fag is a pile of sticks . . .

The other thing was in the middle of king of the float I started to feel like I had to go to the bathroom but I tried really hard to hold it cause I didn't want to miss anything. It was number two so I had to squeeze my muscles as tight as I could down there and it made it really hard for me to come up with an idea of what kind of thing we could do to un-king Jake even though I wanted to cause everybody was coming up with stupid ideas like we should turn the float upside down or like bounce it up and down and stuff even though Jake would still stay on that way. I couldn't even tell them how sucky their ideas were and how Chewy was probably a spy cause all I could think about was that I couldn't hold it anymore or I'd get a stomachache and I didn't know what to do.

But then I remembered how Jake went to the bathroom in the water and if he can do that I can do that too and, anyway, it doesn't matter cause it's like when you're flying off the float and you go underwater, it's like everything's all the same thing so I thought that would be the same for poop too. And everybody pees in the lake so I don't know what the big deal is. I wouldn't have done it anyway if Jake didn't say it was okay the other time and if I didn't really have to go. And besides that I swam way far away from everybody before I pulled my swimsuit down and let my feet float up out of the water and stopped holding it in and stuff.

Jake was right, though. It felt like—I can't even explain.

But then after I swam back, Jake started saying, "Hey, what's that? Hey, hey, guys, look over there. What's *that?*" and pointing behind me and stuff so everybody would look. I bet they wouldn't even have seen anything if Jake wasn't shouting and saying, "Look. Look. Evan just shit in the swim area."

Cause then everybody swam really fast and climbed on the float and started yelling at me and everything so I turned around to look cause how would Jake know anyway cause it was supposed to sink to the bottom. He was right, though, there were a couple of pieces of turd floating around.

Everybody was all grossed out and they dived off the float and swam really fast to the beach to get away from the shitty water but Jake and Chewy stayed on the float to yell what a fag I am and stuff. And just to be mean Jake said, "How are we gonna get back to the beach now, Evan?" He said my name in this really mean way. "We can't swim in shitty water." And I couldn't say everybody else did cause then they would have just been meaner to me. I chased after all the turds I could see and splashed them to outside the net but Jake and Chewy kept pointing and saying "There's another one" every time so I would keep swimming around and around even when there wasn't any left. Jake and Chewy were just making fun of me.

But even though I thought I was gonna cry, I didn't.

I climbed up on the raft after that and stood there all slouchy like I didn't care and I didn't even look at Jake or Chewy, I just looked over at the other side of the lake like there was all kinds of important things I was thinking about that they didn't even know. But even without looking, I could still sort of see them anyway and every time they said anything it was all mean and made everything else in my head disappear.

"That was real smooth, Evan."

"What are you, stupid? You dense?"

"Pud."

"What, did you think shit sinks or something?"

"Fag."

"Pud."

"Fag."

"You stupid fucking fag." It was Jake who said that.

And then they waited to see if I was gonna get all spazzy for them, but I didn't, so Jake acted like he was gonna be nice to me and forgive me and stuff. He said it was too bad I took a shit in the lake cause guess what him and Chewy did yesterday after everybody went to sleep, they went out in a canoe and found those girls and they had like beer and stuff for them to party with and they stayed for like three hours and went out in the motorboat with them and everything. He said how they all went skinny-dipping and how the one girl was sort of fat but with really big boobs but the other two girls were totally hot and even prettier than any girls back home. "We're gonna go back there tonight," he said. "The prettiest one, Becky, whose house it is, is gonna steal a bottle of peppermint schnapps from her dad for us all to drink. It's too bad cause she said she had a crush on you and we should bring you with us, but now what are we gonna tell her?" And I couldn't even ask him what about his fake girlfriend cause I was too sad that I couldn't meet Becky now.

Mr. Schultz came and yelled at us to all come in then cause the water was toxicated or something and nobody could go in it till it got fixed. And even though he didn't say anything, I could tell I was in trouble cause it was all my fault and everybody must have ratted on me after they ran away from the beach.

Jake and Chewy and me swam in and Mr. Schultz made us all

march back to camp and then he told them to go away cause "Evan has things to talk to me about." And then right in the middle of camp where everybody could spy on us and see me getting yelled at he said how he called my dad to come pick me up and how I couldn't even go to the snack bar or leave the camp till he got here and then I was gonna have to go home and all the grown-ups were gonna have a talk to figure out if I should get in bigger trouble like get my merit badges taken away.

I tried to explain to Mr. Schultz about Jake and everything but then I got yelled at about how you shouldn't rat on other people and how he didn't want to hear my excuses cause that's like talking back and he knows what he knows and I have to learn how to respect my elders and he doesn't even care about what happened cause I'm always doing stuff to get in trouble and it's gonna end right here and now.

Even though I was grounded Mr. Schultz made me go get twigs when it was time for the fire and that's when I escaped. Everybody was all busy filling jugs with water and cleaning out tents and stuff like that so nobody was watching me get the twigs. And there weren't any twigs right by camp anymore cause we used them all up already so I said to Mr. Schultz, "We already got all the twigs by camp and the only ones left are still alive and stuff, so can I go farther away to get them? Cause getting ones that are still alive is against the rules." Then, when he said okay, I went out all the way to where nobody could see me anymore.

I didn't even think of escaping from being grounded before that, but now I bet everybody knows I'm gone and I bet my dad's already there to get me and they're all mad and calling me a fag again. But I bet my dad's mad at them for losing me and he's making them look for me and saying how he's gonna sue them and stuff. I bet Mr. Schultz is so scared he's peeing his pants . . .

o　o　o

Since I escaped, I got the idea to go across the lake and see those girls and talk to the Becky one but then I thought Jake and Chewy might be over there too, and they'd get me caught. And the other thing is they probably already told the girls how I went to the bathroom in the lake and everybody would laugh at me, so I didn't do that. I know what I'm gonna do now though and then they'll be scared of me and have to be my friends again. What I'm gonna do is climb to the top of the tower and then take my Scout knife and cut off the foot parts of the ladder. Then I'm gonna tie them back up except not as good in like slipknots or something so after a few times of people climbing the foot parts will get really weak and then start to fall off and stuff. And then whoever's climbing on it like Mr. Schultz or Chewy or Jake, I hope Jake, will fall all the way down sixty feet to the bottom and cry and feel bad for being all mean to me when I'm supposed to be his best friend and then after that I'll come out from where I'm hiding and make him say sorry and I won't even get in trouble from Mr. Schultz cause my dad will be there and Mr. Schultz never yells at you in front of your dad.

Who'll be the fag then? Not me.

Mandel, BG

u32.3691235

A court-ordered injunction will be issued after her mother, attempting against the social worker's advice to fight for custody, presents enough self-incriminating evidence—the girl's emaciated body alone will convince the judge—to ensure that she is barred on the spot from ever seeing her daughter again. She'll be pulled like evidence from their last hug in the courtroom, but not before her mother invokes their private language one last time and whispers a final secret into her ear. The words will make the girl smile. She'll be confused for a moment, believing her mother is playing another of the silly games in which the rules are made up as they go along; she'll know Mommy's sad, and they play silly-billy when Mommy is sad, so she'll wave and her face will gleam. Then as her mother bows her head and turns away, the girl will understand what's happening. She'll let go, screaming as loud as she can, but the walls will absorb the noise and she'll sound even smaller than her little body appears. The first foster home will be meant as a three-month stopgap while a permanent place for her is being located, but she'll stay for less than a month before she is placed in the second, also a stopgap, but this one more accustomed to recurrent bed-wetting and the spitting of chewed food onto the high chair's detachable tray. Here, too, she'll find a way, scratching deep furrows into the antique furniture, to ensure that her stay is cut short. She'll experience brief moments—say, in the kitchen, playing with a hand-me-down doll on the floor as the mother of the house prepares the family dinner—when she feels the urge to babble in a language she vaguely recalls from a time long ago when comforting herself was not such a hard thing to do. She will be afraid, if she gives in to this urge, of being told she must be a big girl, speak English; she must make herself understood if she's going to get what she wants in this world. She will keep mum and instead she will rip the doll's arms off, pull the matted stuffing out of its chest until it devolves into a mass of white fluff and fabric. Her behavior will reach a new depth with each new house, dipping far enough into the antisocial to appall and offend the whole family, to smash the limits of what is acceptable from a waif taken in out of pity and guilt. They'll throw her back into the gap, which will never be stopped effectively—just a whole lot of caulking and no other side, just a conviction that somewhere there's someone who loves her. But she'll have no hope of recalling who that could be. The language will be forgotten.

RED LOBSTER

Our father is in town for the weekend and has decided to take us all out to eat. We've been wigged out all day, racing through our houses in search of our favorite blue jeans and our dressiest sweaters. We are putting on our happiest faces and wondering if he will look the same as we remember him. We can't wait to see him. We've starved ourselves so we'll be ready to pig out. We don't want to disappoint him. We must be ready to have fun—to laugh our heads off, which won't be hard; our father is a very funny man. He makes us all laugh all the time—all except Timmy, who takes Dad's jokes way too personally. When Dad calls Timmy "Tubby," it's funny. I'm sorry, it is. Timmy's face turns red and he gets defensive, and this is funny too. Sometimes we wet our pants laughing, which only makes it funnier. After a while, Timmy starts bawling. He stops being funny when he does this; he becomes obnoxious. He thinks we're laughing at him, but we're laughing with him, we are. We can't understand why Timmy can't just be happy like we are to see our father—God knows he doesn't breeze through too often.

Timmy, laugh a little. We're laughing because we love you. If you can't have fun, we should leave you at home.

None of the rest of us gets upset at our father's jokes. We think they're hilarious. He's always got the newest one about the president's wife. He's got leper jokes, quadriplegic jokes, Helen Keller jokes, everything. You name a topic, and he's got a joke. It's an art to him. We're all jealous; our jokes don't match up. Stevie once tried to get him to pull his finger so he could auto-respond with a box on the ear, but Dad already knew that one; he pulled Stevie's finger and hit him at the same time, yelling, "Gotcha, too slow," as Stevie fell to the floor with a hand to his head. We all laughed, and Stevie laughed too. He said, "That didn't hurt." Later our father taught him how to knock people in the nose by pointing at a make-believe stain on their shirts. Stevie thought this was great and used it on almost everyone he met for almost a whole year. He was still using it the next time our father stopped into town, and they shared a misty-eyed moment over this; Stevie thanked Dad for his parental guidance and our father blushed and beamed, bowed his head.

Stevie gets Dad's jokes, Timmy, and he's three years younger than you, and your mom's prettier. Don't be such a baby.

He picks us up one by one in his new van. When we're all packed in, he stops and dares us to dare him to do a wheelie. We do dare him, but then he hedges like maybe he won't, like it might be inappropriate behavior for a man his age. Timmy, who's a whiz with cars—auto shop is the only class he's ever gotten above a C in— thinks it's impossible; he thinks our father's toying with us and he tells him so. Dad grins at him. His foot to the floor on the gas, he pops the clutch and, to our glee, we lurch into the air. Our stomachs tingle and we come down giggling. Even Timmy's in awe of the wheelie; he hadn't counted on all the motor work our father had done expressly to pull off this trick.

We beg him to do it again. We'd be happy to forget all about eating and just speed around town spinning out on the ice in the grocery store parking lots, burning rubber at stoplights, doing wheelie after wheelie after wheelie and listening to our father tell jokes all night.

He says no, though. We're going to Red Lobster.

Putting Little Petey in his lap to turn the wheel, our father asks Lisa to crawl down between his legs and push the pedals with her tiny hands. He shouts commands, and we bounce, in their creaky control, toward the restaurant. Half a block down the street, Lisa gets confused between the clutch and the brake. She stops abruptly and knocks her head on the steering column, but she doesn't complain and she doesn't give up. She corrects her mistake quickly and has no problem the rest of the way. When she climbs out, we can see that a slight bump is growing under her hair, but she waves our attention away with a laugh. "No pain, no gain," she says. We think that's not bad for a six-year-old who has yet to break her first bone, and we laugh along with her. When Stevie teasingly taps the welt, she refuses to flinch.

Before we go in, our father has something to tell us. It's nothing bad, he says, but he wants to get it out of the way before we're so swept up in fun that there's no room for serious stuff. He corrals us into a corner of the parking lot and waxes ambiguously about the new mystic faith he's been trying to apply to his life. He says it's helping him get himself together. He says he's accepted that he's a simple man who's made mistakes and has many regrets, that he's learned to forgive himself and keep moving onward, that he's learned to live with the fact that life will never stop being confusing. He's not very specific about what all this means, but it somehow relates to the guy with the funny Arab name he keeps mentioning. We don't get what he's saying—it sounds like a twelve-step program to us—but it doesn't matter. We sense how important this stuff is to him and his words are like silk; we tangle ourselves up in them, writhing ecstatically. He finally says something we all understand: he says if he could make all his mistakes over again, he would. We know he means us. He means that he loves us. We can't remember him ever trying to say it out loud before. He says he's going to try to make sure he sees us more often from now on.

Timmy, I'm going to punch you if you don't watch out.

We're all wistful now. Tammy is pale; her body sways like she's about to pass out or run and hide, something she does often when she's very happy or very hungry. Stevie smiles smugly, convinced that our father was looking at him alone. Lisa rubs her welt and giggles with every wince; she's already fond of the memory. Little Petey jumps into our father's arms, where he's bounced benevolently on the same hip we each felt safe against when we were younger.

Before we can sink into deeper realizations about how soon he'll be gone again, our father raises his fist in the air and yells "Charge!" sending us off like a handful of marbles to ricochet through the restaurant doors.

It takes the staff a good fifteen minutes too long to pull enough tables together for us to be seated. We're impatient. Our fun's too important to be slowed down like this. Stevie, unable to get a freebie, rattles and almost breaks the gumball machine between the outside doors and the inside doors as the rest of us squirm, some on the floor and some on the bench by the hostess stand. It's a good thing that our father is already lecturing the manager—calmly but sternly—about how to run his restaurant, because we could easily cause a real scene.

Despite the manager's many yes-sir-right-away-sirs, by the time we're all seated and bibbed our father's face is flushed with anger. He has a right to be upset; he made reservations and they should've been expecting us. Even though most of us will be ordering off the kiddie menu, the bill for this meal is going to be huge. They better go out of their way for us from here on out if they expect to get a tip.

Our father silently mulls over the menu. We can't tell if he's really reading it. Afraid he is sinking, we no longer squirm. We sit up straight, flush against our hard-backed chairs. The worst thing that could happen would be for our father to begin to suspect that we're disappointed. We know how much time he's spent thinking about all the fun we'll have tonight. He's imagined every second and if anything goes wrong we're sure he'll dwell on it until he's convinced the night's a fiasco. Instead of trying to make us laugh, he'll snap at us and at everyone else. We'll all feel responsible. It's already started to happen.

We wish we could think of a joke that would bring him back, but we know that we can't. If any of us tries to talk him out of holding a grudge, he'll only clutch it tighter. There is nothing we can do for him. We are his tiny yes-men and we can't disagree with his moods; they're too delicate for us to carry anywhere he hasn't already carefully placed them. The youngest among us instinctually knows that all we can do is sit up straight, avert our eyes and wait for him to pull himself out of it.

"Okay, gang," he says with a forced, fun-loving tone that strains to keep up with his words. "You can order anything you want, but you have to clean your plates. If you don't, you're gonna have to pay for your meal yourself. I don't make enough money for us to be wasting it . . . I'd give you everything I have in the world but if you throw it away, it won't come back. I'm not a money tree. I don't want you to feel like there's anything off-limits, though. I love you guys—and girls . . . so order anything you want." He smiles wanly.

We breathe a collective sigh of relief. If we show him we're happy, he might snap out of it. Our eyes scamper over the menu as we do our best to find the dishes that taste good but are also expensive. Most of us settle for compromise: the little kids give in to their honest urges for hot dogs or spaghetti; we who are older go for tuna and salmon, shrimp cocktails all around; Stevie, just over the cusp of the kiddie menu, his new adult status still struggling to control the child inside him, settles on a chicken breast sandwich with a side of potato chips and a Shirley Temple—dry. Only Timmy takes Dad's game at face value; grinning with pride, he asks for the most expensive item on the menu—the one that goes by the pound at "market price"—a fresh lobster. He gets to choose it himself from the tank.

That's the way to do it, Timmy. Pick the biggest one.

Our father's eyes twinkle mischievously as, at his bidding, we catch him up on our lives. He listens with an ear to the punny opening, sometimes interrupting the first sentence of our heartfelt explanations of the confusion we feel at sixteen (or six) to twist fart jokes or pull double entendres out of the few words we've managed to say. Except for Timmy, who protests by pretending that his life is perfect, none of us is too disappointed by our father's lack of interest in our, we admit, trite struggles. He picks up a lot despite himself. Last year, when Tammy admitted to sticking her finger down her throat after every box of Corn Flakes she ate, he may have had a joke for every orifice and a lot of funny anecdotes about women and weight gain, but he also, over the course of that long weekend, went out of his way to force-feed her well-balanced meals and whisper in her ear how beautiful she was, all of which helped her try to kick the habit; she's failing, but she's added raisins to her diet and she openly credits him for this. We like him this way; when he laughs at us, he forces us to laugh at ourselves. It doesn't take us long to tell Dad our sagas. They are pretty uneventful; nobody's going through any major turmoil right now. Two months ago, he would have had his hands full with Stevie's suspension from school for the throwing stars and hit list that were found in his locker and Little Petey's escapade through his mom's underwear drawer, but these things have already been cleared up; spring is coming soon and, even if we did have problems, we couldn't be happier than we are this weekend.

Our father launches into stories about his life, which is much more interesting to everyone. His job—somehow related to business or science or medicine or something; we're not sure; each time he explains it, it seems to be different—has taken him all over East Africa. From what he tells us, the people there do very funny things. He says he once saw a car full of government bigwigs in Kenya drive a full mile in reverse before they bothered to turn around, and then they were still on the wrong side of the road! He teaches us the Swahili words for fart, asshole, whore and fuck you, which are all the Swahili words he knows, he says, but he's going to learn more when he goes back next month.

Enraptured, we almost forget to eat. He never runs out of stories, and without the bits of reminder that periodically fall to his plate, we'd be forced to snarf down cold fish when he decided it was time to go. Our baked potatoes would be waxy with recongealed butter. Instead, we chomp along with him, and by the time he's run out of safari tales, all our plates are empty. Lisa, who ordered spaghetti, has even licked hers clean.

Thinking our father might take us to a movie or have a surprise adventure planned for after dinner, we're antsy to leave now. For some reason, he's dawdling. He asks for a refill of coffee. With the tip of his knife, he absently stirs designs in the rosemary-sprinkled grease that's left on his plate. The way he puts off asking for the check convinces us that this is it, that he doesn't want dinner to end; afraid of the separation, he wants to savor us for a while longer before bringing us home.

He takes a short sip of coffee and—his eyes beginning to twinkle again—folds his hands under his chin. Gazing mischievously at Timmy, he says, "You gonna finish that?"

"I did!" Timmy says, as if he knew this were coming.

"Are you sure?"

"I did. I did finish. Everything's been ate!"

"Because if you don't clean your plate, you have to pay your own way. That's the agreement we made."

"I cleaned my plate!"

Pretending to be deep in thought, our father rubs his chin. "Well, okay. I can ask for two checks if you want."

Timmy tips his empty shell toward our father.

"Dad, look, it's all gone! What do you want me to eat?"

Our father doesn't answer. He straightens in his chair and pretends to look around for the waitress.

Timmy has begun to shake. "Unless you want me to eat the shell!" He looks through glazed eyes at the rest of us. He thinks we are all against him now.

"Look, I don't want to argue with you, Timmy."

Our father can't get the waitress's attention, but he doesn't really want to yet.

"I can't eat the shell."

Ignoring this, our father stands up. He cranes his head around as if he's worried that the waitress has disappeared, though she's still less than halfway across the room.

Timmy, don't be an idiot. Hide the shell under the table now, while he's not looking—that's *why* he's not looking! Then, when he looks at you again, lick your lips and laugh and tell him in detail how great it was. I shouldn't have to explain this to you, Timmy.

Realizing our father's stopped paying attention, Timmy gives up his whining. He stares at the shell and periodically blinks away tears. We watch his Adam's apple jump in his throat as he steels himself against the outside world. In slow motion, he picks up the shell, squeezes his eyes shut tight and bites.

Our father sinks deep into his chair in exasperation. "Timmy— hey, Timmy . . ." he says, but Timmy has tuned him out.

We stare as he eats the whole thing, antennae and eyeballs and all.

Meaning to accuse every one of us, Timmy glares around the table, eventually settling his condemnation on our father.

We are all silent. The tears stream down Timmy's pudgy cheeks, but no one will wipe them away.

Our father is watching the mineral flakes spin in his glass of water. He's forgotten all about the check.

Moaning, unable to breathe through his tears, Timmy tries to push himself up from his seat but his muscles give in. He slumps back down and passes out. His head falls onto his plate. Thick saliva, pink with blood, drips down the side of his cheek.

Lisa stifles a giggle. Tammy fidgets in her seat like she wants to steal off for a smoke, but really she's anxious about throwing up on time. Little Petey, thinking Timmy's dead, starts bawling, and our father jumps into action.

With Stevie's begrudging help, he carries Timmy out to the van. We trail behind and, once we're all in, we speed off to the emergency room.

Our father drives like a madman.

No one is laughing.

Timmy is admitted and, after waiting two hours, we still haven't heard anything.

The waiting room's packed and everyone there is insane with anxiety. We're spread out everywhere. We can't keep track of each other. Tammy, thinking we wouldn't notice, disappeared early to sequester herself in the bathroom. Stevie has already nearly gotten into three fights over the seat he keeps getting up from for more candy bars and soda. Little Petey still hasn't stopped bawling. I bounce him on my knee when he lets me, but he keeps pushing me away; he would rather be left alone to pound his fists on the cold tile floor. Every five minutes, Lisa, still proud of the lump on her head, wanders up to a new stranger in her cute six-year-old way and blabbers about how she got it, explaining that she's a lot tougher than her older brother Timmy.

When the nurse finally comes out and calls our name, no one answers. We look around for our father, but we can't find him. She calls our name again and waits a few seconds, her face clouding over with confusion and worry. The aluminum doors swing back and forth for a long time behind her as she disappears to confer with the doctors who've been looking after Timmy.

None of us knows what to do. We can't find our father. He's gone.

Smooth, Timmy, real smooth. He'll probably never come back.

Lapage, Katrina

u32.3691317

The nanny will hold her hand the whole ride up, whispering little tales about her own children's tribulations, about times when they, too, have been kneecapped by crisis and forced to develop their neglected muscles: courage and bravery and suchlike things. The girl will sporadically listen—she'll really try—but self-pity will break up her concentration. Sometimes she'll catch a fragment and giggle or shiver, mistaking pop insights and motherly rhythms for big truths that could change her life. She'll self-consciously repeat the words in her head and she'll wish her mother were there to comfort her, but thinking again, she'll thank God she's not. She'll wonder if the nanny's noticed the coat of fur she's begun to grow since her body began adapting to malnutrition; if anyone's noticed, it would be her. From the driveway, the hospital will look like a fairy palace, even more magisterial than the beach house, and the opulence will make her flinch. She'll tell the nanny to let her walk off the bus alone. She won't have eaten all day. Nor the day before. Nor the day before that. Four days ago, she'll have had exactly ten baby carrots—prepeeled and washed and sealed in plastic for freshness—and, after an hour of picking the sugared raisins and figs out, half a cup of dry granola washed down with a two-liter bottle of spring water. Now, as she stands, she'll be so weak that her legs will shake underneath her stick figure. She won't have had a bowel movement in over a week. Her stomach will begin to tighten with fear, it will shout and kick and protest. Her intestines will soon join in, as if they've been hoarding what little they've received throughout her war of attrition and are now finally angry enough to strike back. The liquid will splatter and stain the back of the sundress she bought special to boost her ego today. As she melts and sinks into the striated walkway, she'll wonder if this is how the nanny's children felt, and she'll know that her mother should be here to see it.

THE GOOD PARENTS

I. Problems Breed Problems

Eventually, after the children had long ago stopped speaking to them; after the children had in fact ransacked and decimated their home in ways that, except for the physical evidence, would never have seemed possible; after Mom and Dad realized that perhaps they had indeed been oh-so-slightly "too permissive" right from the get-go when they had allowed the children to pick their own daily wardrobes, even if it meant that polyester smiley-face shirts would be worn with pin-striped woolen pants just often enough and just late enough in the early spring to force an extra bath, with all the kicking and screaming this entailed, into the children's weekly ritual; after both children had actually gone on bath protest, patiently feigning attention to the endless drone of reasonings—the your-friends-won't-want-to-be-around-yous and the it's-unsanitary-you-could-get-sick-like-that-guy-on-the-streets— but remaining steadfast and assured in the knowledge that spankings were not in the offing, that they would be allowed to sink further and further into their glorious grime, to revel, as children do, in the pungent starch of filth; after the children had concluded that clothes were really a burden they'd rather do without altogether and periodically begun streaking the backyard after the baths that they couldn't *always* escape; after they'd brashly defied their parents' pacifist ideals by fashioning guns from their thumbs and forefingers and playing drive-by-shooting, a game that usually ended with seven-year-old Denali thrashing her five-year-old brother, Zack, with a switch pulled from the willow in the front yard; after the kids had been expelled from school for biting and been put in, then pulled from, therapy because they wouldn't utter a word to the scary bald man; after they'd also begun to destroy things, to set the kitchen and each other's beds on fire along with the obligatory living-room curtains; after even Dulcinea, the purebred, obedience-class-cum-laude black Lab had rebelled, leaving mounds of shit to harden and gradually turn white and crumbly on every carpet in the house—and there's more, but I'll get to that later—after all of this and the accompanying self-hatred, which had grown so acute that they could no longer dodge the word "failure," Mom and Dad finally gave up.

They called Social Services on themselves.

Behind the closed door to their bedroom, Dad stood over the bedside table, trembling, trying to control the burning sensation in his head, the tingle of thoughts moving faster than his brain could process them.

Mom rummaged through the white pages' blue pages. Her fingers shook, ripped and fluttered the thin paper. Her nerves were frenetic and she was afraid, but she did what he asked. She found the ten digits that Dad was demanding and read them aloud.

Dad's fingers shook, too, as he pressed the buttons—it took four attempts before he got the number right.

Only then, as the phone rang five, ten, fifteen, twenty times in some massive building in downtown D.C., did he realize that this was a last resort, the end of his coveted self-delusion. He grappled with the moral weight of his actions for the first time since that summer in Alaska, canning salmon and struggling with what seemed at the time an impossible, frightening task: growing up, making life-defining decisions. Climbing Mount McKinley had taught him the importance of finding the right footholds. One wrong step was all it took to tumble, and it's not like you got a second chance. He'd played things relatively safe, sticking to the easier, low-lying trails. Even then his guide had to talk him through some of the rough patches, but still, there was a harsh, muscular nobility to the act of climbing a mountain, exhilarating and simple. He'd made this the bedrock of his future life. By sheer force of will, he'd sequestered his family high above the worst that was out there—and the worst was everywhere. It wasn't his fault that the worst had crept higher and higher with time. Since Alaska, he'd never stopped watching his feet, so how could he have taken such a wrong step?

His face felt hard and brittle now, tight around his fear. But, no, this was the right thing to do. A man can only do so much when it comes to protecting his family from the degraded society outside his home. There's no shame in crying for help, right?

Mom, the tears swelling and receding like gills, stared at him.

On the twenty-fourth ring, just as Dad was about to hang up in relief, there was a click, an electronic pause, and then the sliding latch of connection. He braced himself. "Hello? Hello, is this Social Services? I'm trying to reach . . . what's it, uh, the department for families in crisis."

Families in crisis. Mom winced. The tears seemed to pour not only from her eyes but also from her arms and her legs and her chest and the base of her spine—from her every pore. She felt like a sponge, wet all over. Gazing at the odd patterns years of chipping had made in the varnished wood of the footboard, she tried to lose herself in the blurry shapes. They could be kittens and flowers and swans—happy things, only happy things. No children, no neighbors, no husbands. But she couldn't stop the shapes from shifting, mutating into darker objects, nameless and dangerous.

Dad patted her on the head and ran his fingers through her hair. He'd been routed to voicemail. As Mom struggled to get away from him, he pressed the button that promised to summon a real person.

Then he was on hold, the computerized voice on the other end replaced by static and classical music.

During those three months in Alaska, Dad had decided that, if he ever had children, he'd raise his kids to emulate the best in human nature, teach them to distinguish between the base and the lofty. Among the many decisions he and his wife had made while she was pregnant with their first child was that they would keep the house television-free. This was Dad's idea, and it was not their only piety. They also banned music unless it was classical or prefusion jazz; junk food of any kind; most types of toys, boy-toys that glorified violence and girl-toys that might teach their daughter to emulate constraining female stereotypes (leaving Legos, Tinker Toys and, with any luck, the children's imaginations). Swearing, of course, was banned even for the adults. To make up for all this severity, the family did things together that other people didn't do. They read *The Odyssey* and *The Lord of the Rings* out loud before bedtime. They told stories around the kitchen table, adding one sentence at a time onto what the person next to them said. On Friday nights they played parlor games — charades, for instance — or the children acted out fairy tales, performed elaborate shadow-puppet shows through a sheet tacked across the hallway. They went to operas and the ballet, to museums where the children, when they were younger, had picked out their favorite paintings so they could learn more about the artists. They took walks just for fun and they knew the names of flowers and birds. The hope was that, by surrounding them with great art and literature, with examples of the heights the human spirit could obtain, and hugging them twice a day like the bumper sticker prescribed, the children would grow into moral, well-rounded adults. These positive alternatives to what

Dad called "the black hole that's popped up to replace our culture" had begun to disappear over the past few years as the children had made it more and more clear that they would rather sit and do nothing than learn about the world. But it was important that they'd started out with this grounding in something more valuable than product placement, sex and violence.

One of the incidental perks of all this was that on Saturdays, with no cartoons to inspire them out of their beds, the children slept late. Saturday mornings were his. All that existed was him and his wife and their bed and the sunrise and their naked bodies. Dad looked forward all week to Saturday morning. Today, he had woken at five-thirty. Kat was still asleep. Her slightly open mouth flecked with wet spit, her dishwater hair, her fleshy forehead that rippled and quivered as if her dreams were struggling to break free—this was all so familiar yet still as mysterious as on the first night they'd slept side by side. He ran his finger over the ripples, pushing them smooth, and she smiled but didn't wake up. He let his finger trail around her eye socket, lazily following the line of her crooked nose. When he reached the slight bump in the bone, he massaged it. The history of her life, her whole personality, seemed to be lodged in this shattered bone. It always got to him. He leaned in and grazed the bump with his lips, letting his mouth linger so he could feel the bone push against him. Sometimes she woke when he kissed her on Saturdays, opening her eyes partway and sleepily smiling as if she'd been waiting all night for this kiss; but today she batted her hand against his face and snuggled her head deeper into her pillow. He wondered what miseries the children had put her through while he was at work this week. He brushed her cheek with the back of his finger and kissed her nose again. Nothing. He kissed her forehead, her lips. He was happy not to wake her.

Pulling back to look at her again, he wondered how she would react if she knew how unworthy of her he felt. It would probably annoy her. He repeated the kisses. It always felt good to kiss his wife, but it felt that much better when she was asleep. He was free to adore her openly; when she was awake, her embarrassment—and the discomfort and shame that this brought out in him—had a way of damping his feelings. He couldn't flaunt the depths of his worship; it was this worship that made her queasy.

Careful not to wake her, he shifted under the blanket, pulling it, a little bit at a time, onto his side of the bed, until she was, almost accidentally, exposed. Now he could gaze at her shoulders, her collarbone. Now he could drink in her breasts. When the children were born, he'd marveled at her breasts and the milk that leaked from them, nursing so much himself that they'd joked about putting the kids on formula. He jumped from mole to mole—together they looked like Cassiopeia—down her stomach until he reached her belly button; it was unusual, another beautiful imperfection, neither an inny nor an outty, but sort of both; it started in and then popped back out, an actual button that he could never resist kissing. His lips crawled over her rib cage and into the softer regions that led toward her abdomen; they left circles of snail trail over her stretch marks and dripped down the weight she had gained and not lost after childbirth. From this close angle, her body had so much variety, rises and falls and changes in color that surprised him the way a mountain surprises—so much more rugged and less uniform from the trail than it looks from a distance. He was falling into a romantic trance.

She twisted and swatted the air, and he stiffened. Don't get too carried away, he thought, leaning back again to give her room. She burrowed her head in her pillow and started to snore. Her personal space seemed to be a tactile thing; he could almost trace the perimeter—far beyond the confines of her physical body—of her being. He wanted to crawl inside this space, to stay here until he was nothing but an extension of her. He kissed her on the forehead again, and as fluidly as possible, he slid on top of her and let his weight sink over her body. He hoped, if she woke up, that she wouldn't think he was trying to invade and conquer. He wondered: How do you explain to the woman you love that there's nothing you want to take from her, that you just want to live inside of her space? How do you explain that it's not her but you that you want to get rid of? To say as much is to sound like you're rationalizing.

Catching the rhythm of her breath, he held his own and waited for the downbeat so he could join hers in unison. The two of them were one, their lives one life. He was the violinist and she the conductor, her breath the baton directing him toward a beauty beyond his comprehension. But when she twitched her nose, he lost the image. Then they were merely two people in a sagging bed, and he was slightly shocked—a shock quickly neutralized by embarrassment, then killed with a mischievous smirk—to realize that he'd been humping her hip. She sneezed and fumbled at her nose with her knuckles. She was still mostly asleep, and as she struggled groggily under his weight her legs seemed to spread and make room for his body. He imagined she must be having good dreams, soft-focus Harlequin dreams in which the two of them spun through pink clouds. Asleep, with the morning light dappling her skin with gold dust, she seemed an entire world—one free from sadness and pain—and he was the luckiest man alive not only to see this, but also to recognize it. He laid his head on her breast and listened to her heart—*bum-ba, ba-bum-ba, ba-bum-ba*—and he wriggled his hand down and pushed himself into her.

Dad hung up and stared at the phone. "You'd think they could hire somebody to—"

His wife spun and stared, wild-eyed as he spoke to her. He tried to hold her hand, but she snatched it away and wrapped her arms around the comforter like it was a lover. Her legs had a nervous bounce to them, and wanting to be strong for her, Dad reached out to smooth her hair. She kicked at him, pushing away across the mattress. She was frantic, just instinct and fear. Her body inched back and back—"Get away. Don't touch me"—until finally she toppled onto the floor.

"What's . . . Kat, no, it's okay. I'll try them again. We'll . . . we'll get through this."

Mom muttered and swore and chewed on her tongue. She lay on the floor and scowled. Dad leaned over to see if she was okay, hoping for maybe eye contact, a brief heavy moment in which she could linger, feel safe, breathe deeply and maybe calm down. But as his head crested the edge of the bed, she spit at him—the saliva arching slowly, fighting gravity, lingering for a half second in the air before turning back to splatter on her chin. She rolled under the bed and began to sob.

Not today, Kat, Dad thought. He didn't say it, though. Instead, he bit his lip and hit redial.

When caught in an untenable situation—and sometimes all this took was rain on a day that was forecast for sun—Mom retreated inside herself toward the moony landscape, equal parts memory, self-mythology and a recklessly free-associative imagination, that she cultivated there. It helped her cope or, at any rate, helped her escape, and since childhood she'd spent a lot of time in this place, hiding from the dense, uncontrollable downturns in her life. Big Symbol Land. She could gaze back across the border and discern shades of meaning that compounded into poignant, epiphanic truths, though these truths were foggy and damp and generally inexplicable to those of us on the other side. Long before she'd met Dad, she had been hospitalized and forcibly taught that the proxy world in which she hid was more dangerous than any catastrophe the real world might throw her way, and since then she'd tried— one day at a time—to stay sane. She still had trouble defining the boundary between healthy contemplation and Big Symbol Land, though; there was no dotted line on the ground, no posted sign saying YOU ARE NOW LEAVING REALITY. The topography changed in mind-bogglingly subtle ways that were hard to notice until it was too late; she suspected, sometimes bitterly, that the boundary existed only in textbooks and on doctors' clipboards. Her way of looking at life wasn't worse—measurably, *objectively* worse—than anyone else's. How could it be? To make judgments about someone's sanity was a subjective act in and of itself. These doctors whose opinions her husband respected with such grave seriousness couldn't prove anything. In *her* opinion, she could do brilliant things with a mind that worked the way hers did. All she lacked was a context in which it might be allowed to run free.

But, no, she had to stay on this side of the boundary, if only to please her husband, for the good of the children. She did her best to show him how "better" she was; otherwise, she knew, he was liable to be up at four a.m. drinking and pacing and drinking. She dedicated herself to the simple, tactile, care-for things moms have historically striven to master. She wasn't good at them, but with determination she'd improve, if only she could keep her mind on the task. And though she knew she'd never be appreciated by her husband, her children, by *anyone*, for who she actually was, she imagined that years from now, Denali and Zack would smile at least at the things she'd done for them—for the grilled cheese and the tomato soup, for the TheraFlu, for the sitting on park benches, bored, watching them climb the monkey bars. Her children would tear up when they tried to fathom her pouring her love into the voids that had grown up to become them.

Her husband, he had the easy job, basking in unearned adoration. He was a mythic figure to the children, a great benevolent giant whose heavy footsteps thundered across the front stoop every evening at six, stirring a frenzy of squeals and a whole lot of yelling—"Daddy's home"—loose in the air. Every day the children darted for the door and stood poised to jump on him as soon as it was thrown open. Each of them would grab a leg, and he'd hobble stiff-jointed around the house, mussing their hair and beaming his star power down on them until he inevitably tripped over one of their bodies and the three of them fell in a pile of giggles. Lying on the floor with them wrapped around him, he'd listen as they babbled on and on about everything—every single tiny detail, sometimes repeated four or five times in their excitement to impart the mass of fun that had happened that day. They'd talk about how they played Bloody Murder, leaving out the part where Mom ran out of the house in a panic, convinced that one of them had been hit by a car. They'd tell him how they dragged the dog by its front paws from room to room teaching it "This is where we go the bafroom and brush our teeth and things like that and this is where we go sleepy time and that's where Mommy and Daddy go sleepy time" and on and on "until Mommy took Dulcy away," of course, leaving out Dulcy's low growls and the way the dog had snapped her jaw as Kat rescued the children. They'd tell him everything, even the ways they had misbehaved, because he never judged, he never reprimanded. He acted as if they could do no wrong, although his eyes darted to her, expressing his disapproval over their heads. Later, when the children were asleep, he'd get the rest of the story and prescribe corrective measures for her to try and fail to accomplish the next day without his help.

And now her failure was total. She didn't blame him. There was something in her that refused to be contained by the days of waking and cleaning and cooking and mothering—this something, this pull toward Big Symbol Land, was at fault. She herself was at fault. It had seemed, when she first met him, that her husband might save her or comfort her or at the very least provide a compelling alternative to the boredom and panic that filled up her days. She'd hoped he might carry her out of Big Symbol Land for good, that his uncompromising morality and noble responsibility would seal up the border. She had been elated and surprised by his unflinching response when she described the horrors of her months in the hospital. Maybe hugs and kisses and his warm sympathy could make the external world more endurable. So she fumbled and stumbled beside him for years until, now, she knew he was as cold as everything else, and that even if he were Prince Charming, he couldn't save her from herself. She just wasn't programmed to operate by the world's circumscribed standards. She was a terrible parent; today's events proved it. Why *not* disappear into the safety, the comfort, of her own pathology? The doctors were wrong: anything's better than this.

And easier. Freer. More natural. There was no reason to rein in her thoughts, to track them and judge them and strangle them into a logical sense, taxing her brain and spinning in circles until her head was so jumbled, aching and tortured that she couldn't think at all anymore. Better to go with the flow, wherever it took her, even into the world of terror and wonder.

Mom shut her eyes and played with the weave of the carpet under the bed. She stepped into the pitch-black darkness inside herself and floated there untethered. A white light, a dwarf star, flickered in the distance. Voices hung heavy around her, almost as if she could touch their vibrations, but they came in slow and shaggy and she couldn't make out the words; she knew their tricks, though—eventually they'd tighten and start to taunt her. She briefly lit on her familiar hope that this was the tunnel leading toward death, and she half expected to see her life flicker past in rewind as she began walking toward that dwarf star. But no, that was just wishful thinking. Big Symbol Land was in fact not the sanctuary she told herself it was. Danger crouched everywhere waiting to pounce. She lived in fear for a reason. The world was crazy and from here she could follow its deepest logic.

She fled further in, slipping her focus toward muscle and bone, her hair, her blood, her womb, this physical thing that was and wasn't her. She tried to concentrate on the tiniest, cellular parts of herself. Remembering how she had learned about these things in Science class, back when she was going to grow into someone important, she saw her cells—little sacks of jelly, somehow adhering to each other—adding up to her. This had awed her then and it awed her now; something like God—whatever that is—was mirrored in her body. It was the unknown, and the unknown was holy. Her body. They could regulate her mind, but her body, that was something else entirely. It had incubated her two children, it had taken single cells and, through a process so much like creation, transformed them into complex, breathing, living things. Her husband and the doctors couldn't take that away no matter what kind of mojo they played.

The voices in her head rose out of the murk. *But we'll get at your body, we'll get that too, we'll do things that you can't imagine, you'll see what it's like to have nothing, to be nothing, you'll see, you'll see.*

She tried to sink still further, her muscles relaxing, allowing the bones to burrow. She felt sore. It wasn't her imagination and it wasn't the voices or the void. Something had happened earlier this morning, somewhere between sleep and waking. She had been dreaming when something—it was her husband—had poked into the place that was now sore. She'd bucked and flailed and then something had popped and she'd woken up to discover her arms and legs spread for this man's body, probing and dripping all over her depths. This really happened. She had relaxed, played dead, stared at the door, which, thank God, was shut. He hadn't taken long, he never did. Just a little suffocation until his heavy gut relaxed and he made that ugly groan and the globby spume of mucus squirted into her. Then he turned and his hipbone stabbed into her thigh. He'd gazed at her and smiled, so proud of himself— as if he were a five-year-old innocently waiting for Mommy's pat on the head.

The voices again. *Yes, and the children. What about the children? Don't lie, we know when you're lying.* This morning the door had cracked open and two eyes showed vertically, one above the other. She'd seen them, she was sure. All of this since then had merely been proof.

The voices would not quit. *And you did nothing. You did nothing. You failed.* These voices, they were even worse than her husband.

Dad was now getting busy signals. He'd reached the point of repetitive action and put his fingers on autopilot: hang up, hit redial, hear the tone, hang up again. When he tried to remember why he was calling, he couldn't. Without Mom's support, he was losing his nerve. His thoughts kept wandering over to her. It was just like her to turn a situation that should bind them together in perseverance into an excuse to throw a fit; everything was always all about her. He wished she'd come out from under the bed. He had to keep reminding himself, think about the kids, that's what's most important. But his focus was split, now, and he couldn't concentrate. He put down the phone and collapsed on the bed. He picked up the phone again. Redial. Disconnect. Redial. Disconnect. Redial.

Mom heard a cracking in the wooden brace that held the mattress up. She gasped and watched the bed sag above her. This bed was too old for them to be sleeping on. It was too old for her to be lying under. Look, there were bloodstains and semen stains and breakfast-in-bed stains and this was the flipped side, the other side had been on top since Zack was born, before they gave up housekeeping. The springs had dyed the threadbare fabric with rusty circles. Her voices were telling her, *Finally, you'll be set free.* It could happen any minute now, the wood splintering into barbed phalanxes piercing her skin and lodging in her vital organs, the mattress entombing her there on the bedroom floor—a fitting end.

And of course her husband had chosen the weakest spot to sit on. He was trying to kill her—just like he'd nonchalantly been doing for years now with all of his shrugging disregard for quality time and his yammering on about moral integrity and society's wrongs, and then there was the real him who had clawed into view today with a sloppy good-morning rape, that's what it was, rape, as if the rhetoric he'd built their lives on had really been nothing but words. But what he didn't know was that she was untouchable, impervious, because she didn't care; he could kill her, fine, she looked forward to it.

But it would hurt, warned the voices.

Ha. Not as much as it would hurt him—because this is a suburb, and when they hear the sirens, people come to gawk from blocks away. It would make the local news, the state news, it might even slip into D.C., and before he knew it his crimes would go national. Pundits would turn them political. The story would come out in tabloid detail—MAN KILLS WIFE WITH BED; KIDS TORTURED MOM WHILE DAD WAS AT WORK; LIVING IN FILTH (WIFE WAS A DOMESTIC SLAVE)—and he would be condemned by the very world he judged so harshly. Considered the emblem of an evil, selfish man, he would have no champions. And she would be martyred and sainted, and in her grave she would no longer have to pretend to agree with his every half-baked, elitist opinion. The best part was that he would become everything he stood against: a media spectacle, the gossip of his life pawned off on the masses as if it were news, as if it were profoundly disturbing and more than just another drop of entertaining trivia to be added to the public's supersaturated consciousness.

Let him kill you. Show him how cold his heart really is.

Mom sobbed. "I loved you," she bellowed.

Dad bounced the phone in his hand. "Kat . . . Kat, can we, just . . . one thing at a time."

"And you had to ruin it."

"Kat, honey, really, I'm . . . How am I supposed to . . ." Dad's voice went almost to a whisper. "I don't know what to do." His head hung low and defeated from his shoulders. He rubbed his scalp. Redial. Disconnect.

The sound Mom made seemed to come from somewhere deep in her bowels, a rumbling, groaning howl, and Dad rubbed his palm down over his face. He pulled at his mustache and beard, wiping the weakness and self-pity away like crumbs. He flushed red. "You know? I mean, can't you act like an adult just this once, just today?"

When Mom finally spoke, the words were drawn-out throbs of sound. "You. Raped. Me."

Redial. Disconnect. Redial. Disconnect. Redial.

Dad was back on Mount McKinley, higher up now than he'd ever climbed. He fumbled for handholds, hoping the shadows in the rock face didn't lie. He was exhausted and still he could not see the summit. He'd never reach it; his only two choices now were to admit defeat or climb until he fell. The air was thinning. He climbed, though he no longer wanted to, and his body grew heavier with every vertical foot. Below him he could see a jumble of fir trees, each one a spear aimed at him. The terrain began to spin. He wanted hot cocoa, a fireplace, the fraternity of strangers united along an uncomfortable wooden bench, comparing versions of their shared adventure. He wanted to be at the point in the future where you get to brag about what you've accomplished. His fingers were numb. There were blisters on his feet. He wanted, most of all, to let go.

And at that very moment he finally got through. He heard the ring, but not until after his fingers had pressed the wrong button and hung up. He shouted, "Fuck!"—swearing for the first time in years—and hurled the phone at the wall. The plastic mouthpiece cracked. The wiring snaked out. The microphone drooped toward the floor like a dying sunflower. Except for the sex, the memory of which his wife had just ruined, this was the first thing he'd enjoyed all day.

He listened to Mom sobbing under the bed. The sound was deep and meditative, like a prayer. When she spoke again, her voice was low and distant, an echo in search of freedom. "Where are my children? I want to hold my children."

Where were the kids? He didn't want to know, but he stood up anyway. He wasn't sure what he'd do when he found us. He was still falling.

II. Where Were the Kids

Where were we? Loitering, terrified, eavesdropping outside their door. We didn't know what we'd done wrong. We knew it was something, though, a monumental something. But what?

As we did nearly every Saturday, Denali and I had tiptoed across the street to Suzy's house that morning to watch cartoons. The bottom section of her split-level had been converted into an adult-proof playroom with smurf-blue shag carpeting and smurf-blue walls on which her mother had painted hot-air balloons and clouds and helicopters and miscellaneous other flying things. We didn't have anything like it at our house: the beanbags and blow-up chairs, the sleep-away couch, all the old furniture left after her mother's divorce; the long fluorescent lights; and the toys strewn everywhere—Atari cartridges, stray Colorforms, marbles from the Chinese checkers game no one knew how to play, more than one Etch-A-Sketch, even those huge Nerf bopper things, expressly made for kids to pummel each other with. She had an Easy-Bake Oven and a Snoopy Snow Cone. She had Starbrite. Her Lite-Brite's color pegs were strewn around the room like tacks. She had both the male and female Monchichi monkeys, and they could suck each other's thumbs. Toys upon toys upon toys. You could find a toy or a toy component tangled in every strand of carpeting. Just close your eyes and plop your hand down: there was a plastic high heel or a tiara belonging to one of the numerous Barbies, or maybe, Custard, Strawberry Shortcake's cat. The playroom at Suzy's house was a shrine to everything my sister and I weren't allowed to have, complete with cable TV and a VCR.

Cartoons came on at six-thirty, but we usually arrived around seven. We'd kneel at the tiny ground-level window and peer down into the room, squishing our noses on the glass to search through the grime for Suzy. If she was up, she'd be sprawled on the floor, sucking her thumb and kicking her bare feet against the frayed couch cushions. Hearing your rap, she'd shift on her elbows and take a long last look at *Super Friends*. Then she'd suck the juice off her thumb, drawing it out slowly with a smack of her lips, and wipe it dry on the carpet. Scratching her bottom, she'd roll over and wave us to the front door. We'd sprint around and wait for her—she always took her time—and listen until she jumped for the top lock. When the door opened we'd clamor excitedly into the house, the screen door, its spring broken, banging behind us. The same every time. Suzy would put her finger to her lips and pucker, hissing a stream of spit through her front teeth as she shushed us. "My mommy's asleeping," she'd say. But we'd already be gamboling down the stairs to gape at the magical screen—entertainment for hours, until just before nine when we had to run home and pretend we'd just woken up.

Oh, the luxury of these two hours. To loll every which way on those beanbags or couch cushions or, best, in Suzy's big round papasan chair—a satellite dish you could sit in—imagining ourselves out trolling for trouble with the Garbage Pail Kids or reshaping ourselves as more daunting, less frightened creatures—shiny as chrome—while we saved the universe with the Transformers. Even the Care Bears my sister and Suzy adored so much were captivating; I wouldn't admit it to them, but the gauzy safety of the land of Care-a-Lot and the Forest of Feeling got to me, made me all mushy inside—something about those rainbows. It didn't matter what we were watching, the momentous thing was that we *were* watching, breaking the taboo—and without any negative psychological effects. No, TV was helping us. Though we wouldn't have been able to put it this way, we knew, we just knew that if we logged enough surreptitious hours, the massive assimilating force behind them would shove all our weirdnesses and eccentricities into a cellar where no one could see them. We'd put an end to the whispers, the jeers, the abrupt pointed silences. The condescending questions—from adults and children alike—that ran along the lines of "What, are you some kind of Jesus freaks?"

It would take a lot of catch-up, but we were ready, and when Suzy, our sympathetic friend, was in the mood, we could get her to tell us what we'd been missing. She'd already begun to teach us about prime time. When we'd mastered that, we would tackle daytime. Then the grown-up shows that came on after bedtime—even kids who owned TVs weren't allowed to watch them. Eventually, we hoped, we'd be so on top of the current season that we could move on to TV history, sneaking peeks at reruns of what we'd missed, though Suzy said the best shows—the ones that were canceled after thirteen episodes—would be lost to us forever and that we'd probably never catch up, what with cable and all-new, never-before-seen episodes of one or two or sometimes a whole bunch of essential shows every single day.

She quizzed us during the commercial breaks. This morning, just like every other, we had done miserably.

"Who's on *Family Ties*?"

"Um, that guy from that movie. Uh . . ."

"I know it, Michael A. Fox!"

Suzy rolled her eyes and bopped me on the head with the Nerf thing. "That's who he is in *real* life. Who is he on TV?" She banged it impatiently on the ground and clicked her tongue. "I told you before."

"I know it. I just have to remember." My sister twisted at her eyebrow. "A. It's an A name."

"Al-ex!" Suzy sing-songed. Then she bonked each of us on the head. "That's so easy!"

My sister crossed her arms and pouted. "If you let me think! I knew that—"

"*Chip 'n' Dale's Rescue Rangers!*" Suzy shrieked.

We were transfixed.

At the next break, Suzy snapped right back. "Who's on *Charles in Charge*?"

"We haven't got done with *Family Ties*."

"No, cause you have to do *Charles in Charge* cause it's more real to life and there's girls more our age in it."

"I never heard of *Charles in Charge*."

"Uh-huh, cause I told you before, memember? It comes on two times: on Saturday on nine at three and on Sunday on five at six?"

My sister clawed out of her sprawl on the couch and, coiling sullenly into a ball, dug her chin into the palms of her hands. "No, you didn't."

"You just don't memember."

"You never told us."

"Cause—"

"Cheater."

Suzy stuck her bottom lip out in disbelief.

Denali struggled to make herself clear. "You're trying to make it so I think I'm stupid."

"I told you before—you just forgot."

"Nut-uh."

"Yeah-huh."

Throughout the repetitive argument that ensued, Suzy periodically glanced at the TV, and when Chip 'n' Dale returned, she disengaged with an uncanny nonchalance—just a "humph" as she flopped toward the screen. My sister tried to follow her cue, but she was too angry. She kept turning back to say, "Nut-uh cause you never did." This wasn't helped by Suzy's under-breath chides (so quiet she could deny them) of "Yeah-huh" each time my sister appeared to be over it. At the end of the show, as the credits flashed over a frozen frame of Chip flying a biplane, dragging Dale behind him by a frayed rope, they lunged right back in where they'd left off and kept at it until my sister broke. "I don't care. I don't care about stupid *Charles in Charge*—"

Suzy bit back a smile and glanced at me from the corner of her twinkling eye. She crossed her legs Indian style and primly seesawed on her hands. "*Ed Grimley's* on!" she said. The half hour tolled with the opening chime of another theme song.

Maybe if Suzy hadn't been so gleefully triumphant, Denali would have been content to sulk. Maybe she would've just glared at the TV and brooded about Suzy's cruelty and selfishness. Instead she threw out a challenge. "I know stuff you don't know too," she said.

Suzy spun around—"Shhh"—and then back in time for the first line of dialogue.

"I know what mommies and daddies do when they go sleepy-time."

"I don't have a daddy." Suzy's voice was chipper.

"Zack knows too."

Suzy gazed at the TV, oblivious. She giggled at Ed's silly dance for a moment, then scrunched up her pudgy face and shouted, "Rerun!" raising the remote and aiming around her head like a hot-shot sharpshooter to zap the channel.

"I haven't seen it," I said.

"Zack, remember what mommies and daddies do?"

Seeing me pout, Suzy started to sing. "This is my house / This is my house / I get to watch / What I want."

"Zack, don't you remember?"

"Shhh—*Mighty Mouse*."

I wanted to disappear. With little inching motions that I hoped would go unnoticed, I sank lower and lower into the papasan's cushion and watched Suzy watch the cartoon. She giggled at the artisan mice scurrying through the quaint town, fear and anxiety playing on their faces, hammers and anvils dropping behind them. They gazed at the sky and prayed for Mighty Mouse to rescue them.

"You have to be not wearing any clothes to do Mommy and Daddy sleepy-time things. Remember now, Zack?"

I tried to pull myself up, but the papasan's basket tipped and the cushion slid out from under me. I toppled to the floor, then flopped onto my stomach and propped myself up to stare at the TV as if I'd done all this on purpose.

"Tell her, Zack?"

I shrugged my shoulders and kept my eyes fixed on the screen.

"Tell her—tell her what we saw."

"They . . . yeah. Were doing stuff." I picked at a Lite-Brite peg caught in the carpet.

Suzy was unimpressed.

Denali's gaze hopped from the TV set to me to Suzy. "Okay, fine, I'll show you." She pulled her pink t-shirt over her head, kicked off her bobby socks and stretch pants, then yanked her panties down and flicked them onto the pile.

I'd seen her naked numerous times, when we'd been shoved together, under duress, into the bathtub and then when we'd streaked across the backyard in attempted escape. Even so, I was shocked. Previously, there had always been some other obscure yet immediate danger commanding my attention. Now—with the fluorescent lights of Suzy's playroom casting her nakedness into high relief—my sister's body itself seemed dangerous. And this pointed toward a frightening thought: maybe the hugging and kissing and rubbing we'd seen through the crack in Mom and Dad's bedroom door that morning was the dangerous thing we'd run from all those times before.

"Zack, take off your clothes too."

I heard her, but also didn't hear her. There was nothing inside me with which to answer; I was too busy gawking—as Suzy was—at my sister, naked and belligerent in the middle of the room. My eyes tingled. My vision blurred. I didn't want to be naked like that. I didn't want Suzy and my sister to examine *my* hairless body. But also, I sort of did, and I didn't know why, which made me not want to more; it felt like fingers were picking through my skin and dancing up inside, probing, trying to yank I wasn't sure what from me and then I would be without it forever.

"I can't do it all by myself," said Denali.

Suzy clobbered me with the Nerf thing. "It's not fair if you don't play."

The commercials were segueing back to the show with a bubbly Casio rhythm. My sister and Suzy were huffing and wheezing. Suzy emitted a slight popping sound from the back of her throat every time she exhaled. The fluorescent tubes crackled. The whole room arched toward me expectantly.

Standing, I pulled down my shorts, then pulled them back up. I unvelcroed my shoes, yanked them off and pulled down my shorts again. I held my breath and I pulled down my underpants. My t-shirt hung to my thighs. I dawdled. Suzy yawned and my sister scowled. I closed my eyes and imagined that I was alone as I pulled my t-shirt up over my head.

"You have to take your socks off too."

My sister and I stood across the room from each other. I wondered what she and Suzy were seeing as they stared and stared at my body. I studied Denali's belly button. The more I let myself contemplate her, the less I worried about their contemplation of me. This helped me ignore the way my skin was telling me exactly where they were looking.

My sister directed.

"So, cause I have to lay down like regular sleepy-time. I'm gonna . . . like that, all sprawly, and you have to be on top of me . . . not like that . . . not like that, either. You're too far to the side . . . No, Zack, you have to come this way."

"If you throw up," Suzy said, noticing the sick look on my face, "you have to go to the bathroom first, okay, promise?"

"No, not *there*! Zack! Do it right! Umph—I can't breathe! I can't breathe!"

I rolled to the floor.

As Suzy's interest gravitated back toward the TV, Denali's face flared purple with rage. I remembered the time she had whipped me with the willow branch and I searched the room for something to push this thought from my mind. Easy-Bake Oven. Snoopy Snow Cone. Dried clumps of Play-Doh the size of hand grenades. Girl toys were scattered everywhere.

"Just do it right, Zack!"

Suzy flipped the channels.

"Suzy, no. Suzy, watch." Denali splayed her legs, and following her orders, I pivoted back and forth on her hipbone. "See, Suzy? Like sleepy-time stuff."

"I seen that before."

"Zack, you have to make the noises."

"No."

"You *have to*! Make the noises, Zack. Like 'un-n-ngh' and 'uh-uh-uh-aaah' and like that."

"I seen that on TV."

"Do the noises, Zack! Now!"

I grunted feebly.

Suzy was won over. "You're doing *it*!" she shrieked.

"No, Zack, go more faster."

"You're doing *it*!"

"First slower, *then* faster. And then more and more faster—don't you remember? And I have to look over at the side like I'm sad and stuff."

"That's *it*! You're doing IT!" Suzy pounded her Nerf thing on the floor in glee.

Denali glared at her suspiciously. "You never seen this before."

"I did on TV, but never for real."

My pelvic bone was sore. My back ached from Denali hitting me when I made mistakes. There was a pressure and pinching in my groin as I teetered over my sister. Most of all, my stomach hurt. It occurred to me that this was no fun, but also that none of us were watching TV. It was just there, making noise in the background, flashing purple and red, green and yellow. It was just there, like Suzy's mother was there.

For the first time in the many weeks since we'd been sneaking over to watch cartoons, Suzy's mother was there in the playroom. Her hair was bent and knotted, weirdly cowlicky. She shielded her eyes and squinted as she stepped into the blaring light. She blinked at us, not really looking, then blinked at the TV, then blinked again at us. Her expression changed, tensed and puckered.

Suzy, her mother, Denali and I were all petrified, our bodies leaning away from each other like we were at the top of a roller coaster. The moment would come soon, we didn't know when— right when we decided maybe it wouldn't—for us to descend at a rattling speed. Suzy's mother lunged and snatched my sister and me by the wrists. My back scraped the length of the molded wood banister. My ankles bounced and burned against the five carpeted steps to the front door. Suzy's mother kicked at the screen door and, as it snapped back, it pinched Denali's forearm. She screamed, and Suzy's mom kicked the door again and again, bouncing it off the aluminum siding until finally she'd wrangled us onto the lawn, tripping, spinning, ashamed of our nakedness, dragging us behind her as she sped across the street and plopped us like trash bags on our own front stoop.

Juggling our clothes, Suzy chased after us. She was crying. While ringing our buzzer, her mom picked her up and straddled her on her hip, innocently, tenderly.

Suzy's wails drowned out her mother's words, but the contextual clues were raw and her meaning was unmistakable. The way her eyes constricted into taloned crow's-feet. The way Dad stared off with his nose in the air, as toward the frontier, like he was trying to make out the ferocity of the storm that was about to overtake him. The way he flinched and took it as she continued hammering him.

Dad nodded gravely and raised his hand, a silent plea for mercy. A strained lipless smile passed across his face.

Suzy calmed to sniffles, and her mother ran out of things to say. She readjusted her daughter on her hip and just stood there in contempt.

"Thank you," Dad said. "Thank you for telling me. I wouldn't want not to know. We'll . . . we'll talk to them."

"I think it's more than talking that they need."

"I . . . yes. Well. Thank you. We'll . . . take care of it."

Still, Suzy's mother refused to leave. I wished that I had some clothes on.

"Really . . . we can handle it from here. Thanks for bringing them home safe though, um, sorry about all this."

"What," Suzy's mom said, "is *wrong* with you people?"

Dad pulled his thin lips into a smile and nodded his head, imploring her to understand, please, be kind now, to please go. Shielding her bloodshot eyes with her free hand, she reluctantly staggered back across the street. Suzy, her mouth pressed to her mother's bathrobe, peered back at us and flapped her fingers goodbye.

Then Dad ushered us into the house and around the half wall to the living room.

There was Mom, looking frightened and lost, in the rocking chair—creaking back and forth, a coil of tension. She noticed nothing.

"Look what the cat dragged in," Dad drawled weakly.

In our own ways, we all understood where she was. She'd been there before—was almost always there.

Dad barked directions. "Go get the phone book, Kat. Kids, get some clothes on—now. I don't want to see you do anything—nothing, understand?—until we come out of that room." He pointed toward their bedroom. "We'll talk about this later."

III. Mom and Dad Grow Up

So here we were, Denali and I, in oversized t-shirts, crouching for the second time that day outside their door. Making funnels out of our hands, we held our ears to the wood to listen. We could hear pacing. Muffled and tense conversation. The foghorn bellow of Mom crying. And then that single intelligible sentence: "You raped me." I wasn't sure what it meant, but I knew it was something incredibly bad. "Is that what we did?" I asked Denali, but she punched me and hissed, "Shut up," which I guessed meant yes and explained why I'd felt so queasy while doing it. Something smashed against the wall, and when Mom sobbed, "I want to hold my children," I wanted to shout out, "Yes, hold me, Mommy. I'm scared too," but that seemed like a breach of a different sort. Anyway, my sister poked me — "They're coming" — and we scurried off to find some innocent thing to pretend we'd been doing while waiting for them.

Dad, reeling from Mom's accusation, and fumbling for something to moor him in place, picked up the pieces of the phone. Everything seemed unfamiliar to him, slightly shifted, the perspective skewed, diced and cubed, and he wasn't sure when or how this had happened. Three syllables from someone known to exaggerate shouldn't have the power to shake a man of dry, stoic principle. The phone, though, with its cracked plastic casing and exposed primary-colored wires, was tactile, simple. If he didn't know how to fix it, at least he knew how he had broken it. He twisted the wires farther from the casing so he could study the workings inside. Guessing where the dangling mike might fit, he tried to wedge it back into place and roughly stuffed the wires around it. He snapped the batteries into their compartment. Meticulously straightening the antenna, he tried to knead out every kink, but the dents, like cracks in ice, extended with agitation and it broke off. He gave up, placed the phone into its cradle and lumbered out of the room.

Where were the children? What further havoc were they wreaking now?

Slowly, so slowly, he moved down the hallway. This was a new depth of degradation. This was a place of self-loathing. He fell and fell. The details of what had come before this instant—his children's actions, his wife's, everyone's—had been left up above on the rock face, replaced by a cold, burning sensation.

Denali and I sat cross-legged, silent, thumbing through magazines—*Omni*, *The Utne Reader*. When Dad appeared at the edge of the room, we overreacted—too much surprise, too much teeth in our smiles, the conspicuous, false cheerfulness that only a guilty child can muster. We tilted our heads and gazed up at him in an adoring, approval-begging way we had learned from our dog. But he ignored our plays on his sympathies.

He seemed twice as big as himself and he watched his feet as he walked. His body jerked like a car with a faulty transmission, staggering forward, in constant danger of freezing up. Finally, he sank to the fireplace hearth and sighed.

"Hi, kiddos," he said.

A saggy, tired look of love crossed his face as he finally looked up.

I've been trying to understand this from Dad's point of view. I didn't have one of my own at the time; I was too young and was still moving forward. And if I've been flip, if I've been unfair to him, it's only because I can't fully erase the version of this story Mom later taught me to believe. I'll try to be better now and look at Dad from a less biased perspective.

You could have called our family a social experiment. Dad was trying to lead us through to the next step in evolution. As much as this came from his philosophical beliefs, it was also a political act; for Dad the two were intertwined. He was convinced that all people were equal, that we were all on a journey that—if only there were quality education and truly equal rights and compassion and help for those who still couldn't take care of themselves— would lead us to enlightenment, a universal respect for life, a better world. He aligned himself with the underclass but wanted them to be more like him, like the person he'd turned himself into. He couldn't see this, of course. He thought of his politics as liberal and social, but he disapproved as the disenfranchised and cultur-ally diverse masses swarmed onto the radio and TV and filled the air with a hundred conflicting backbeats. In truth, his politics were culturally conservative: he believed everyone should strive to live like the elite of yore. Thus, his bias against pop culture and his attempts to educate us in the great musty art of the past. Liberal in thought, conservative in deed.

He approached personal affairs Socratically. To his mind, mistakes came about through philosophical misunderstandings, through selfish ignorance of how we are all connected, because someone forgot to consider the effects of his or her actions. He was good at noticing this when it went on around him and equally good at neglecting his personal role in its happening, at standing back and sniping at anyone near enough to show their weakness, teach-ing them how to be stronger and better and more enlightened, all without ever admitting that he himself might also be partly to blame.

And right here, on this one day, I think, Dad's contradictions finally broke.

"So, what do you kids have to say for yourselves?"

Nothing but puppy-dog smiles.

"You don't have anything to say? Do you even understand what you did?"

Denali answered. "We were watching the TV?"

I tried my best to keep smiling.

"Watching the TV. This is funny, huh? You think this is funny."

"No."

"Why are you smiling, then? Why are you smiling? You kids, you act like you live in the jungle. It's going to stop. You don't even understand what I'm saying, do you? Right now . . . it is going to stop." His face got red, and he jumped to his feet. "And wipe those fu—shi—dang smiles off your faces before I smack them off."

What went through his mind in that instant?

Did his thoughts pause on his attempts to get through to Social Services? Did he wonder about the home life of the counselor he'd wanted so badly to speak to? Did he compare himself to her? His lily-white self, whose one or two dabbles in drugs had been truly recreational, part of a search for enlightenment? Did he think about the stories he read in the papers about the unwed mothers in the projects where there was no heat except when their children, no older than his, brought down on themselves a sort of heat that didn't warm the house but left it colder? Did he make the connection between the Department of Social Services—across the river in D.C.—and the reports from the devastated neighborhoods there? He lived in the suburbs, in the upper-middle class, where the walls of his life were padded. Did he realize how infinitesimal our problems were, really, when compared to those Social Services dealt with each day? Did he realize that his quacky beliefs about the best way to live didn't make our lives better, they just made us seem like cheapskates and freaks? Did he realize how condescending it was to the poor American underclass for him to forsake the American Dream of winning by having the most toys? And did he understand how immature it was of him to throw a tantrum and destroy the phone just because they hadn't dropped everything to save his white ass?

Maybe. I don't think so, though.

I think he was too self-absorbed to do any of that. I think he was blaming us, his two rugrats who just wouldn't learn and who just didn't care, who at their young ages had already fallen into depravity. I think he was wishing we'd never been born because then his life would still have had structure. I think he was regretting the faith he'd had in his wife's ability to transform her life. I think he was beginning to believe she would've been better off in the psych ward, doped up, lobotomized, locked away from this world that was capable of hurting even sane people like him. I think he was trying to expel his anger and self-pity.

And that's why he grabbed my sister so roughly and pulled down her panties and buckled her over his knee. That's why he hit her and hit her with his open palm. That's why he was out of control for the first time since his Alaskan enlightenment.

Or maybe it was because he loved us. Maybe it was because he knew he was wrong and he couldn't lock us away from the world regardless of how ugly that world might look. Maybe it was because, in lieu of reason, he knew only his own father's manner of discipline.

I think, maybe, he wasn't thinking anything. Maybe he was just feeling the depths of his failure, and the wild beating he was giving Denali really did hurt him more than it hurt her.

I watched as Dad's hand swung down and Denali winced— spank, wince, spank, wince, spank, wince, like a machine, the parts repeating the same motions over and over. I imagined what it was going to feel like when he got to me. It would sting at first, but then feel numb. There'd be pinching where, bracing himself, he roughly gripped the baby fat under my armpit. Bright red welts would appear on my behind, and they would ache for days.

Denali screamed, a sustained high pitch. But for all that noise, she didn't struggle.

I wondered how many times he'd have to hit her before he was sure she had learned her lesson. Was he counting? And would he hit me the same number of times?

If I'd been swift, I would've run for some nook or cranny in which to hide, but I couldn't move. I was stunned and confused and felt somehow deserving of my turn. I knew what we'd done wrong now. It wasn't watching TV, it was the other thing, the one that had felt so dangerous at the time. I'd raped Denali. Or she had raped me. Either way, I was dirty and in need of punishment.

But before my turn arrived, Mom put an end to it. I've tried to understand her perspective on all that happened, as well. Somehow, while Dad spanked Denali, Mom had tried her arm against a much larger foe, herself, and miraculously she'd won. When she stormed into the room—at least for that moment, that day—she seemed to have ripped the tongues from her internal tormentors and escaped the country where they'd been holding her. Years of analysis hadn't been able to achieve results like this. Dad's shower of love, the padded room he had tried to create with his high art and classical music—none of this had helped her find a way out. Now, here she was, victorious, livid, back in reality.

"Stop it! No more. Don't touch my—you're gonna have to get out, do you hear me? I'll kick you out if you lay one more hand on my daughter."

He froze mid-swing and Denali squirmed out of his grasp and waddle-ran to her bedroom, slamming the door on us, five, six, twelve, fifteen times until I heard the wood begin to splinter and the hinges begin to pop.

"I mean it," Mom said. She prowled warily around the room, shooting looks at Dad, growing stronger and saner as the minutes descended like rain.

It was as if they'd changed places.

Dad was a figment of his haunted past now. He stared at his hands. His face twitched. Alaska no longer existed. Or not the Alaska that had changed his life. The one after which he'd christened his daughter, the one that had taught him to see, was gone. Now there was flat land and big sky and wind. Now there was only a slushy plain through which the little he could make out in any direction was the same empty nowhere offering no escape. Watching his footsteps and testing the rock, rappelling and choosing the daunting, more treacherous, fulfilling path, he had arrived at the wasteland he'd been climbing away from. He should have known. There is nothing but wasteland.

He hid his face in his hands and cried.

"Come on, get dressed," Mom said, steadying her palm on my head. "Tell Denali to get dressed. We're going to Best Buy."

Defeated, resigned, his emotions flaccid, Dad swept his bleary eyes across the room until they came to rest on Mom.

"To buy a TV."

Nothing could touch him, not even this. He bowed his head to her, nodded and shrank.

I scurried off to Denali, but she wouldn't open her door.

"Denali," I whispered, "Mommy's gonna take us to go get a TV."

I waited.

"Come on, we get to help pick it out."

I waited and knocked and waited and knocked.

"Leave me alone."

"But, Denali—"

"I don't care."

Putting my clothes on alone in my room, I let the smile crack over my face. We were going to Best Buy to purchase a TV. Our lives would be better now.

As Mom and I left, she called over her shoulder, "If you want to, you know, you're free to come with us," but Dad was still surveying the mess he'd made. He stayed behind, shivering, confused, lost.

IV. And

After the TV was bought and the cable installed and the dog shit cleaned up—the dog itself in fact carted by Dad to the ASPCA against the rest of our wishes—after the broken phone had been fixed, and my sister and I had been marched across the street to offer the sheepish apologies that Suzy's mother refused to accept, after our family gave up on chore lists and Mom went on Wellbutrin and Dad stopped trying to teach us right from wrong, and Mom and Dad stopped having sex, stopped spooning, even, clinging instead to their carefully apportioned sides of the bed—after all that, our family finally began to resemble something a lot like normal.

There were no more house fires sparked out of boredom. There was no more drawing on the living room walls with crayons. No more Bloody Murder. No streaking the backyard or sneaking off to see Suzy. We never exposed family secrets again. No, we became good little children, my sister and I, humble and meek and scared of our shadows. We walked in the light with our heads down.

Other things disappeared, too. Dad gave up taking us to art museums and orchestra concerts and the ballet. Homer and Tolkien disappeared from our bedtime rituals. The voices in Mom's head seemed gone for good, as if pushed out by those that climbed into our house through the TV set. She gave up crying, but she also gave up smiling. We didn't jump Dad and drag him down to our level when he arrived home from work anymore, instead we just shrugged and fought over the remote control.

We stopped hugging each other.

During the six years it took Mom and Dad to finally decide to separate, Mom watched TV like an addict. Now she does Human Resources, censoring the real-life soap operas in Atlantic Republican Bank's credit-card department. Dad remarried immediately after the divorce. He and his new wife do not have children, but they do have a television set; his house is cold, as encrusted with frost as tundra. Denali came out of the closet three years ago, and though I wonder if what happened this day might have had some bearing on how she turned out, I haven't asked. I don't understand her. My mother, my father, I think I know them. From my sister, I am estranged.

Steele, BB

u32.3691252

When she's clean enough to reminisce, his mother will fill him with stories of his father's rage at the powerful, elusive forces that had kept him down, of how he'd been haunted by what he imagined they'd eventually wring around his black neck. She'll tell him how she was so afraid of loneliness she'd let his father take this rage out on her. And about how his father had left her without warning or reason anyway. When she's not clean, she'll barely speak to the boy. She'll sway and nod on the sofa, half eyeing the television with the glassy eyes that look more fake than those falling off of his stuffed frog. Or she'll throw things at him because he's young, because he can't do anything without help. He'll be scarred here and there, mostly nicks—but this one time, playing caretaker, she'll have a spatula slick with hot grease. She'll be turning bacon, an entire package, turning and turning already burnt bacon, obsessively focused on the soothing repetition. He'll tug at her shorts and ask what's that smell. When she kicks him, muttering under her breath, he'll say, "Mommy, it smells like burning and lookit, the smoke, and I'm scared, Mommy, maybe the building's afire." Turning and not seeing his moist wide eyes, she'll bring the hot aluminum down on his back. Grabbing his nappy hair, she'll bring it down on his back. He'll twist and writhe as she keeps on smacking. A blow will hook skin with the tool's blunt edge and then he'll be bleeding like he's just been knifed—four inches long right below the collarbone, it will look like they went for his heart and missed. He won't be doctored but she'll go to rehab, shocked straight from the sheer horror of it. When people ask, he'll blame it on the father, who he'll say had tried to kill him before taking off to find some other mess. He'll tell the story so often that it will become true. Chilling one teenaged day, smoking a blunt in the park, he'll tell it again to some sad-eyed old guy. He'll like the guy. He'll ask, what's his name, sounds familiar—it will take a second, a delayed reaction, the blood hanging back so it can clot with rage. Sizing the old man up, he'll contemplate murder but the sad eyes will sway him against it; there's no way those eyes could rail against the world, hurt a fragile woman or stab their own son. The boy will save his urge for when he gets home, but by then he will have lost the nerve.

SHE RENTED MANHATTAN

The blue-and-white-striped sweatshirt, or the ribbed off-white sweater from the Limited, the Guess jeans or the short skirt with black tights, maybe the other Limited sweater—the one with the pocket sewn on at the hip—or the maroon lamb's-wool one she got from Benetton for her birthday, she could wear it with the tan Banana Republic pants . . . but she doesn't want to be too dressed up.

Mary can't decide. There are too many choices. There's no way to tell which one's right. Although all the clothes in her wardrobe imply "Mary," each item reflecting at least a tint of the bright attitude she tries to have toward life, there are minutely calibrated differences in how they affect her mood. The wrong combination of wardrobe and mood has her crawling out of her skin, thinking, "This is not me," or "This is the wrong me," or "This is an impostor—pay no attention—she's just trying to give me a bad rep." With the right combination she feels sexier than she believes she actually is, or smarter, or more fun-loving, or less afraid to leave the house.

She wishes she knew who would be at the party. Living outside the party loop, Mary usually doesn't even hear about them until the Monday afterward. Stephanie said this one's supposed to be big, but who knows, it might be an all-girl thing. If she knew there weren't going to be boys, Mary would just wear a hooded sweatshirt and the new jeans that still need to be broken in. But how could there not be boys? The entire town knows that Sarah's parents are in Florida and she has the keys to their lake house.

Mary's nervous stomach tells her to dress defensively, just in case people she doesn't want to talk to—like Justin—show up. She wishes she could wear her ripped jeans, a white pocket tee and the white leather vest that, when she bought it, seemed like such a risk, so capable of labeling her a girl not to be messed with.

But tonight, she remembers, it's supposed to be cold. She returns to her closet. She starts from scratch.

Today is Mary's birthday. At exactly 2:36 this afternoon, she turned sixteen. Except for the hour out to eat with her parents at the Olive Garden and the half hour during which Stephanie stopped over to deliver her present—a heart-shaped crystal jewelry box that Mary has already filled—she spent the day alone. She rented *Manhattan* and dreamt of being Mariel Hemingway all afternoon.

Mary loves *Manhattan*; those first few notes of *Rhapsody in Blue* draw her into a world so moody, both romantic and melancholic, that by the end of the film (it's in black and white *on purpose*, so it's a film) she's convinced that if she were a girl from the Dalton School she would finally be a legitimate person. She's always imagined that the refined and sophisticated Manhattan so casually captured by this film is far superior to the small Wisconsin town into which she has had the bad luck of being plopped down; Manhattan's a place where life is not cheap and people are careful to insulate it with bubble wrap—visiting psychiatrists for extra padding and considering the effects of their every action before doing anything stupid. And *that girl*—to Mary's blunt mind, a girl like the one in *Manhattan* could never experience the complete, disassociative wrongness that makes up Mary's idea of herself. Yes, Mariel Hemingway is the epitome of everything Mary is not and should be. When she strolls through *Manhattan*, Mary knows it's where she was supposed to live. This knowledge has a way of cheering her up. She is able to be less ashamed of not fitting into the mise-en-scène she belongs to, that of Goodrich High School.

Nonetheless, not fitting in is intensely lonely. Mary sometimes imagines that the only life she has is the one she vicariously experiences through Stephanie. Stephanie's life is exciting. Mary often gets no phone calls for a week, but Stephanie's phone never stops ringing—even the catty clique that decides their school's public opinion sometimes calls her. She's always chock-full of gossip, and no matter how bad Mary knows gossip is, she revels in her almost palpable thrill and shock as it's invariably passed along. Listening to Stephanie, Mary almost feels bold herself; Stephanie isn't afraid of anything; she talks about her dates more flippantly than Mary would ever dream of—Mary has gone out on a few dates, but they're *never* as exciting as Stephanie's; they're always too fraught with emotion.

Stephanie sometimes drags Mary out into this larger world, and tonight she's given her no choice. That's how she phrased it this afternoon: "You don't have a choice." And Mary gave in. Anything—even a terrifying party she knows she's not wanted at is better than moping around the house watching the seconds stand still on the kitchen clock and imagining how much fun the girls who go out with football players are having, how excited the skateboarders must be by whatever misdemeanor they've defiantly chosen to pull off tonight, imagining even that the ostracized, the hackers and computer game addicts, are together, celebrating a new CD-ROM with schnapps from someone's parents' liquor cabinet. Mary can't stand another night of that—not on her birthday.

Soon, after she's chosen her outfit, Mary will wait on the front steps of the duplex her family shares with the Hildebrandts for Stephanie's Escort to appear down the street. She'll watch the sky darken from blue to gray and fret about what might happen tonight.

When Stephanie finally arrives, Mary will immediately ask if the outfit's alright. If it's wrong, Stephanie won't be afraid to say so. If need be, she'll even wait as Mary changes. They both know how clingy Mary gets when she feels insecure. Then they wind up resentful, not speaking for days, both wishing Mary was less of the person she is.

But tonight, although Stephanie has minor qualms with the jewelry and thinks Mary's makeup is a little too much, she will merely say, "Take off the hat and you're perfect." Baseball cap thrown into the house, Mary will amble back to the car and they'll be off.

As always, Mary will jump, first thing, into Stephanie's day, asking hundreds of questions, hoping to get every detail of every second since last time they saw each other. Normally, Stephanie savors the attention, spouting off the mendacities of her life like she's a charming and charismatic world leader holding court to a worshipful audience on matters of global importance. Tonight, though, because Mary refused to come to Milwaukee shopping, and because it's Mary's birthday, Stephanie will want to hear about Mary's day first.

Mary will play coy, like she would tell if she could, but she's been sworn to secrecy, until Stephanie gives up in frustration, lightly teasing Mary and making her promise to tell all later. Mary will cross her heart and pray to God that Stephanie forgets about this, that her self-pity is allowed to wrap itself silently into the past the way guilty pleasures are supposed to. Then she'll press Stephanie to get on with the litany.

She'll listen raptly as Stephanie starts in on the traffic jam caused by some kind of accident involving a jackknifed semi on Highway 41. She'll take mental notes as Stephanie rates, song by song, the cds that she bought at the Grand Avenue Mall. She'll commiserate and say, "You're not fat, though, it's okay," as Stephanie berates herself about the humungous salad, with mega-amounts of grated cheese and ranch dressing that wasn't even low-fat, she ordered at T.G.I. Fridays—she ate the whole thing! Stephanie will describe every pair of clam-diggers and every designer t-shirt she didn't buy for summer clothes with as much fervor as she lavishes on those she did, and Mary will passionately agree with her choices. She'll shiver as Stephanie vividly re-creates all the details of the nagging, half-spoken argument her parents dragged from retail outlet to retail outlet, and then all the way home in the car.

Camping up her disappointment to heighten the guilt, Stephanie will ask Mary why she refused to come along. Mary won't know how to explain that she has more fun listening to Stephanie describe what happened than she does when she actually goes out into that world, where she feels so heavily pressured to be spontaneous and fun that her self-consciousness clings to her like plastic wrap. She'll meekly attempt to shift the conversation in a different direction.

And because it's Mary's birthday, Stephanie will begrudgingly let it go at this first sign of bristle. She'll fly into gossip, reeling off names and vital information like who's broken up with whom, who's started going out with whom, and who's likely to fight with whom over all these intrigues. The list will go on and on.

It will seem to Mary as if every single student at Goodrich High

School except her is somehow involved in a steamy affair or a messy divorce. At first she'll consider herself lucky as she attempts the impossible task of keeping all these sex lives straight, but the chart in her mind will quickly grow unreadable. Laughing, enjoying the geometry of the project, she will make Stephanie backtrack and retrace and define the length of each amorous line. Eventually, she'll realize that everyone has been with everyone else and she'll wonder how she was so sadly able to keep herself completely outside of the matrix.

She'll wonder if it's her own fault. Stephanie would say so. "Toughen up, you've got nothing to lose," she'd say. They've argued about this before, and now Mary's always sensitive to the possibility of Stephanie turning on her. It won't surprise her—she'll have almost been expecting it—when Stephanie's grip on the steering wheel tenses in the extra-safe ten and two o'clock position and she lets the car coast to an illegally low velocity, as if preparing for falling rocks ahead.

Mary will allow the gossip to tumble away on the pavement behind them and wait deferentially—flinching—for the lecture that she sees coming.

As the car falls to an inch-along idle, Stephanie, with a beleaguered look pulling at her face, will glance back and forth between Mary and the street. She'll glance at the ranch houses lined with manicured saplings. She'll sigh, shoring up her energy, and say, "So tonight, when you're at the party—"

Mary will tense and search for a distraction—the hard plastic bow-tied koala bear hanging from the rearview mirror, the chewing-gum wrapper crumpled on the dashboard, the frayed, growing hole in the foamy hand grip tied around Stephanie's steering wheel, the colon blinking between the hour and minute on the dashboard clock. She'll cut Stephanie off—"No, I'll be good. I promise. I'll be good"—as she becomes transfixed by the blinking, the blinking, the blinking.

Stephanie will press the brake and the car will jiggle to a

stop in the middle of the street. She won't even bother to pull off onto the shoulder. She'll contemplate the windshield and rapidly pop her jaw. Then she'll turn and attempt to make eye contact.

Sensing Stephanie's effort, Mary will focus more tightly on the blinking colon.

"I'm so serious, Mary," Stephanie will say.

And Mary will try her best to ignore her.

"Mary. I know you're listening, Mary. And just let me say that this is really stupid. This is really baby-ish. Because, Mary . . ." Stephanie will pause expectantly. When she starts up again, her voice will contain a tinge of whine. "Why won't you look at me? You don't even know what I was going to say. I wasn't even gonna say anything bad."

Mary will be drawn in by this. "Yes, I do know."

"What, then?"

"That I better not act like a spaz."

Stephanie will arch her eyebrows and say, "Well . . . but I wasn't going to say it like *that*." Trying to turn it into a joke they're both in on.

Mary will turn to the window and study a sprinkler's rotation across the lawn beside her.

"I was going to say it's your birthday, Mary. Do you think I'd drag you to a party where nobody liked you on your birthday? I wouldn't do that. People like you. You're not an untouchable. Skanky Stacey and G. I. Joe, they're untouchables, but not you. You just have to be yourself tonight, Mary, please? Just be . . . Relax and let things happen and don't look at people like they're like offending you when they say stupid shit. Just talk to them. They all want to be your friends."

It will strike Mary that Stephanie's being completely sincere, but she won't acknowledge this. Instead she'll remind herself of what she knows: that to be known is the biggest danger there is, to be known is to risk being hurt. She can't prove this and there's no way she'd share it with Stephanie, who would want proof, failing to comprehend how Mary or anyone else could know something simply by knowing it, as if by osmosis, without even an anecdote to back up the conviction. Mary will sink into the rhythm of the sprinkler, tuning out Stephanie's pep talk. She'll wait, frozen in place, until Stephanie gives up in frustration, revs the engine and squeals off toward the lake.

As she watches the houses grow farther and farther apart, gradually being replaced by alfalfa fields, Mary will skim backward through the events of her day until she reaches *Manhattan*. She'll let herself wander into a game of compare and contrast, pitting herself against Mariel Hemingway. Mariel Hemingway would never find herself fighting with her best friend on the way to a party she didn't want to go to in the first place. Mariel Hemingway would just refuse to go. She'd be too busy doing actually interesting things with exceptionally fascinating people: engaging in intellectual debates; going to the theater and watching real actors, *famous* actors, as opposed to the plant managers and town council members and mothers on view at the community theater productions Mary herself is privy to; reading books that were written by people she actually knows. And gradually, as this imagined life unfolds, Mary will replace Mariel Hemingway with herself.

Every light will be burning in the two-story house. People will be huddled in packs all over the lawn and especially around the keg on the back porch. A cluster of kids will be sitting on the dock with their shoes off, swinging their feet in the water, daring each other to be the first one to skinny-dip. Couples, thinking they're hidden, will be necking in the shadows of oak trees and maples.

Stephanie will jump from the car and run around blabbing to everyone that it's Mary's birthday, and even though Mary knows she's doing this to get back at her for the fit in the car, she won't mind. No, she won't have time to mind, she'll be too overwhelmed by the reactions of her classmates. People will come to her of their own volition, just to say happy birthday, to find out what she's been up to, to *chat!* And when Mary answers their questions with ambiguous, wholly uninformative responses, they'll be satisfied. They won't think she's weird. They'll accept her. Wow! She'll smile, half embarrassed, half elated by the attention.

Greeting her, Sarah will tell her she "shines." Mary won't even think about running to the bathroom to search her face for the blemish that might have provoked such a witticism. Instead, she'll blush even more and return the compliment with neither paranoia nor skepticism. Soon, enough people will be fawning over Mary that Stephanie will leave her on her own and drift into the crowd across the lawn. Pumping another beer from the keg, Mary won't even notice she's gone.

Normally, Mary can't think of anything to say at parties. They feel like exercises in masochism to her, and when trapped in them she sinks toward an isolation so deep that her own voice sounds like it's talking down to her. Most of the time she leaves early. When she stays, she drinks herself dizzy attempting to push herself into a more sociable state of mind until, by the end of the night, she needs help walking and has to be carried home by someone she vaguely recognizes as Stephanie. Tonight, surprising herself more than anyone, she'll drink just enough to maintain a nice buzz.

Slightly mystified, tingling with the sensation of winging it, she'll speak casually with people she's always thought were stuck-up about their plans for the summer. Without betraying how incredibly disconcerting she finds it, she'll listen as they bad-mouth people she's always thought were their best friends. She'll even toss out a few nasty crowd-pleasing comments herself, which will be no less satisfying for being unintentional. At some point she'll realize that Stephanie has wandered off, but instead of inspiring the usual panic, this will be simply an observation, giving her no more pause than any of the other random things that flit through her mind: "It's sort of interesting that everybody smokes Marlboro Lights" or "I think I just stepped in spilled beer, oh well." Tonight, Mary's life will have the soft-lit feel of a romantic movie and, for the first time she can remember, she'll compare it favorably to *Manhattan* and let herself fall into a deep, cozy joy.

Sometime near midnight, she'll take a deep breath and the air will smell perfumed and sweet. With a sudden desire to feel the night breeze, to get lost in the blanket of romance it conjures up in her mind, Mary will wander off alone along one of the wooded trails that meander past the house on their way around the lake. Still within earshot of the party, she will find a boulder that juts out into the water and, hoping there's no poison ivy, she'll forge off the trail to climb onto it.

Sitting with her knees to her chin, her plastic cup of beer tucked neatly into the crook beneath them, Mary will marvel at how the surface of the lake shimmers like a robe of white gold in the moonlight, almost as if it could be unhooked from the black water below and folded away, to be brought back out only on special occasions, when the moon wants to wax romantically at someone who can appreciate the subtleties of its beauty. Mesmerized by the white gold, she'll lose track of time and space, to be brought back only when Justin calls out from the trail behind her.

"Sarah said you were out here somewhere. Are you hiding or something?"

She'll look over her shoulder at him. "No . . . I like the quiet here."

"I was looking for you." He'll sound embarrassed.

She will smile and curse herself, remembering how much she likes him.

Mary and Justin went out for three weeks in January. They

never really did anything, mostly sitting on the concrete wall behind the gym during basketball games and wandering around Franklin Park on weekday nights when no one else was there. They hardly even made out, maybe five or six times tops, and even then she only touched him a couple times through his jeans—and he never tried to go further than massaging her breasts lightly and sucking her nipple once after midnight as they rocked on a swing in the park. Mostly it was just sloppy kisses and long, beautiful conversations. Justin seemed like a die-hard romantic. One night, after talking on the phone so long that they'd both grown tired and incoherent, he told her they shouldn't hang up, they should sleep with the receivers next to their ears and it would be like they were in bed together. "I'll cuddle the phone," he said, "and pretend it's you." She had thought they were falling in love until he inexplicably stopped calling and got his sister to say he was never home. He pretended not to know who she was in the hallways at school.

Justin is smart *and* good at sports. He floats around between all the cliques, so even though he's not technically the most popular guy in school, he's actually more popular than the most popular guy. One of the things Mary hadn't understood when they were together was why he wanted everything to be such a secret. He'd said it was because if everybody knew how much the two of them felt for each other, it would end up as gossip and their feelings would begin to get warped and diluted; their feelings would belong to everybody else as much as they belonged to him and to Mary. To make him happy, Mary had kept the relationship a secret even from Stephanie. She'll remember, now, how she had felt like bursting with no one to talk to about either her happiness while they were together or her confusion afterward. She'll remember how she'd felt manipulated and secretly humiliated for weeks. She will put this out of her mind, though, as he asks if it's okay for him to climb up and sit next to her.

She'll nod and scoot over, taking a sip from her beer. She'll be conscious of how sweet her face feels from smiling as she watches him come close to losing his balance in the trench of mud between the trail and the boulder, grabbing and almost breaking a nearby sapling just in time. As he scrambles up the side of the rock, he will almost spill his drink—some kind of fruit juice concoction, probably vodka and cranberry. She'll take it from him and suck a long draught through the straw, not giving it back until he settles down next to her.

He'll grin like he doesn't know what to say.

"Look at the water, doesn't it look like it's almost got skin?"

He'll stare gravely out at the lake for a while, then nod. "Uh-huh."

"Or maybe not skin, like a coat or something . . . you know what I mean?"

"I wanted to say happy birthday."

She'll smile again. "Sweet sixteen—yeah, right." For a moment she'll ponder the danger involved in continuing the conversation. "Did I tell you that? I mean, before?"

"Sure."

He'll reach out to take her hand.

They will sit in silence, watching the water lap lightly against the boulder.

She has desperately wanted to know why he stopped calling, but she'll refrain from asking, afraid that his answer might vandalize the story she's constructed to explain his actions. She figures he ran from his feelings because of a fear of overload, a fear of desiring more than he could hold on to; he wasn't ready yet to test his own boundaries and she can forgive him for that—it's only human. She can still like him this way. If he tells her his side, it might contradict this.

Gazing at him, she'll try to catch his eye, but he'll be transfixed by the water. The expression on his face will be so sad and distant that the urge to kiss him will be hard to resist.

"Was it good?" he'll ask.

"What?"

"Your birthday."

"It was okay. I watched *Manhattan*."

"What's that?"

"A movie. You probably wouldn't like it. It's black and white."

"Did you like it?"

"Uh-huh. I've watched it every year on my birthday since I was about twelve."

"I'd like to see it, then," he'll say, squeezing her hand. She'll squeeze back and massage the soft spot beneath his thumb. Slowly, the two of them will reach for a kiss. She'll take his lower lip between hers, lick it, and then, pulling a few inches away, blow on it softly, kiss him again and nestle her head up against the tender part of his shoulder between the neck and the blade. She'll think about movies and moonlight, about people in love in their own little bubbles with nothing outside of the frame of their film.

After a while they'll wander back to the party. Mary will hold Justin's hand, unafraid of being seen, and guide him along the path so he can continue to examine the treetops.

As they come out of the woods and move across the lawn toward the house, Mary will realize how late it is. The handful of people left will be sitting around in half-drunken stupors, trying to sober themselves up for the drive home. They will be negotiating rides and complaining about how stale the beer has become.

It will seem to Mary that she and Justin are in a world separate from that of the party, as if they are seeing their friends from a distance, as if high school's meaningless, not worth her fear, not worth any consideration at all.

When Stephanie sees her, she'll tell Mary that she was worried she'd gotten lost or fallen, drunk, into the lake or, truthfully, that she'd had one of those panic attacks and was quivering under a tree somewhere.

Mary will smile abstractly and say that she's fine.

Stephanie will go on and on about how she wishes Mary had let her know there was nothing to worry about. When she notices Justin standing there, her whole demeanor will suddenly change, and she'll flash a fake smile and offer him and his friend Mike a ride home.

Mary won't pay much attention to any of this. The broad smile still on her face, she'll gaze at everything glimmering under the lamp in the front yard, finding patterns in the minuscule grains of glass that seem to float in the paved driveway, virtually tasting the dew that clings in perfect circles—each one enclosing a tiny diamond of reflected light—to the grass.

She'll climb into the back seat, squeezing up close to Justin, who will put his arm around her shoulder.

They'll make out for a while, rubbing their cheeks together like seals, nibbling each other's lips, brushing each other's teeth with their tongues.

They will giggle conspiratorially when—as the car bounces over potholes—they are jolted apart or their foreheads and noses bump together.

As the car heads onto the better roads in town, Mary will let the rest of the world disappear completely. To her, the back seat of this Escort will be all there is, she and Justin, alone in a velvet-lined pocket. She'll awkwardly shift her weight to one side and work her free hand gradually down Justin's chest, finally resting it on his belt buckle. With just a tinge of trepidation, she'll check to see how turned on he is.

Leaving her hand on the bulge in his jeans, she will look into his eyes.

She'll think of all the things they didn't do during those three weeks in January and wonder if the things they did do had meant anything to him. He said they did at the time. They had in-depth conversations about the difference between getting sexy with someone because you mean it and getting sexy with someone just because they're there. They both agreed that it must feel different when you mean it, although neither had the experience to back up this conviction.

Justin will scrunch up his nose and squint in a goofy way.

She'll wonder what Mariel Hemingway would do in this situation. She would be bold. She'd be scared, of course, but she'd still go where her emotions led her. That's what it is to be sophisticated: to walk through the world like there are no rules holding you back.

Still staring into his eyes, Mary will begin to move her fingers slowly up and down like a snake charmer.

He'll slide his own hand under hers and fidget with his belt. When he has it undone, he will unhook the top button of his jeans. He'll stretch his hand up behind his head, then change his mind and brace it against the door, moving it every few seconds until finally—scrunching up his nose again—he'll rub her cheek with his knuckles and hide his arm, up to the elbow, behind his back.

She'll finish unbuttoning his jeans for him. As she takes him out of his underwear, she'll try to remember how they describe this in the tasteful "massage" books and how-to books on her parents' bookshelf. She'll look down as she begins to massage and tickle the length of his penis with her fingertips, and trying to invoke in her memory the illustrative line drawings of naked people with seventies haircuts, she'll flick her finger back and forth across the tip like the wrong end of a magnet swinging in and out of his field of attraction.

When she leans up to kiss him again, he will open his eyes and study her face through weighted lids. His pupils will be dilated, his irises almost not there. He'll scrunch up his nose and roll his bloodshot eyes in self-mockery.

Mariel Hemingway, Mary will wonder, how far would she go

for love? She'll twist her body around, bending at an uncomfortable angle, her elbow digging into his chest. She'll take him into her mouth.

He won't moan. He won't gasp. He won't breathe heavily. She'll have to crane her neck to see his face. He'll bite his lip in an ecstatic grimace, then, once she's turned back to his penis, he'll gyrate his hips and run his fingers roughly through her hair. A few times she'll gag and, trying to be subtle, pause and gulp down air and adjust her mouth.

She'll wonder where that feeling—the romance and soft light—went.

When Justin abruptly pushes her away, she won't know how much time has passed. The look on his face will be cruel and judgmental. The slight alcoholic buzz will be flushed from her blood by racing red cells that burn in her face like shame.

As she slides across the cracked seat away from Justin, Mary will notice that his friend Mike is looking back at them, shaking his head. Stephanie will be driving intently, as if her peripheral vision has been forcibly blocked off.

Justin will slip his underwear up and over his still-hard penis, quickly button his jeans and buckle his belt, then turn completely away from Mary to watch the street glide past out the window.

They will drop Mary off first. Crawling out of the car, she'll want to say goodbye to Stephanie, but the look she'll receive as she opens her mouth will stop her. Stephanie will stare until Mary can't bear it. Lowering her eyes to the curb at her feet, she'll faintly hear Stephanie's flat "Happy birthday" as the car rolls away down the street.

Mary will watch them turn at the corner, then stare at the empty street. She'll imagine what Justin is saying: "She wanted it." But no, she doesn't, she wants that other thing—the romance, all the gauzy, riled emotions she's sure she would find if she were in *Manhattan*. She'll look at her clothes and think, "This stupid Benetton sweater, it's too big. This stupid shirt with its stupid fake-pearl buttons. And this stupid silk bra, and these stupid jeans—as if Guess even means anything." She'll feel more naked than if she actually were.

But right now, Mary can't decide what to wear. She wants to pick just the right thing. She wants to be someone—anyone—else tonight.

Erasmus, Noah

u32.3691384

He'll gag and heave, but his parents will force him, twice a day, to swallow, and eventually he'll appear healed. It will feel like drowning, sinking and swimming, being pulled backward as if he were caught in a riptide, the weight pressing down and compounding despite his frenetic flipper kicks, his heart-shaped breaststrokes, his hyperactive thrashing. Then he'll be under, the light refracting, the surface receding as his system fills up with Ritalin. The furrow of concentration concealing his sleeping mind will seem to his parents a vast improvement over unrelenting kinesis. He will bloat in all this water. His voice will not sound like his own. Through some hydraulic illusion, magnified by the ever-growing ocean between him and the self that's submerged in this chemical saline, the world will appear to him boring, its edges dulled just like his. Without the sensory overload, the so-much-out-there, the awe-inspiring everything worthy of his fascination—when chasing a squirrel doesn't lead within seconds to picking paint off a fence, maybe eating it, then digging for earthworms and making mud pies to throw at the squirrel from on top of the fence if he can get up there without falling and hurting himself, all performed at such a manic pace that the only thing that can keep up with him is the running "Mom, hey, look, Mom" monologue by which he narrates his ongoing adventures—with none of this worth the effort anymore if it means swimming impossibly against the undertow, he will be completely manageable. He'll get used to it: this is the way life is supposed to be.

MERCY FUCK

She was barely into puberty when it started—twelve, she told me. One day she was playing Mommy at her Fisher Price stove in the basement, and the next she was in the living room doting on the men, fetching them beer, and she couldn't fool anyone, not even her mother, into thinking she was still some innocent little girl. Or that's what it felt like. Maybe there were a few interim years of sitcoms and soap operas, raspberry lip gloss and bubblegum eye shadow—she must have learned somewhere—but in her memory there is no transition: she was first one thing and then another, innocent and then experienced.

I prodded her. "What do you mean? You were only twelve, you *were* still an innocent little girl."

"I'm only seventeen now, and am I an innocent little girl?"

"I don't know, are you?"

She glared at me and popped her jaw.

She wasn't innocent. Not now, not when she was twelve. Naive, maybe, but no, not innocent. She blushed too darkly when her uncle said things—and not from embarrassment. Well, maybe the first time, but not after that. "You've got yourself a knockout, there, Teddy. I'll tell you what, hey, if I were you, I'd keep her locked up until she's twenty, thirty, forty-one. Until she's an old bag like this one." He slapped his wife's ass as she walked by and was swatted away, his wife barely annoyed, as if he were a common fly. No, even at twelve, she liked the attention too much. She coveted it. She liked the thought that she might be a dream, a figure of beauty, floating like Mary the Mother of God far above the world of men, casting shame and neglect on the lumpy women they could actually get their hands on. The bawdy directness with which her uncle spoke of her, the implicit fear and explicit rancor that her overwhelming femininity provoked, were normally reserved for the women in beer commercials, the women in thongs and wet t-shirts who, on the posters and calendars hung in the basement, lounged on the roofs of cars, not the real, mango-shaped women who lived on her block. He said to her father, "You're lucky I saw her when she popped out, or I might be tempted to forget she's related," but he was staring right at her, his eyes lazy under heavy red-rimmed lids, and she stared right back, locked eyes with him and thought for a moment about whether it was better to cross her arms in embarrassment or throw her fists on her hips, arch her back and show off what was growing so disconcertingly quickly between her shoulders. She chose to hide her new body, but still, her father had sensed the transformation and sent her off to change her clothes.

"Where'd you get that halter top?" he asked. "I never gave my permission for a halter top. Go put on something floppy, a sweater, something."

"Dad, it's summer."

"So?"

"So . . ."

"So nothing." As she scrambled up the stairs, he slapped her ass just like his brother had her aunt's.

Later that night, the relatives gone, her father got lurchingly drunk. Big deal. What was news was what he did in the haze before he passed out.

I was sick of this story. It was ruining the mood. We'd hooked up around eight and since then had been wandering all over town, visiting friends she just had to see. Boys, always boys. I didn't know any of them. She lived in the next town over, smaller and less sophisticated than mine, though that wasn't saying much, my town was all rust and dust itself.

We hung around first in a damp, cluttered basement and swilled beer with three geeky kids who were playing nickel-ante high-low, anaconda, fuck your neighbor. They didn't even bother to nod at us when we walked in, just kept playing, muttering about how much the party they weren't invited to tonight sucked and how the people going were the same assholes they didn't want to hang around with anyway, fabricating great tragedies in which those who slighted them now, while in high school, turned out to be failures once they were released to the real world, where nobody cared how well you could throw a football. They called each other dickweed, numb nuts, fucking mo-fo whenever a hand was won. She asked how to play a few of the games, five-card draw and the one where everyone got a single card, held it to his forehead, bet, then on the count of three, looked at it. They shrugged. Their leader—who had the balls to wear an unbuttoned Hawaiian shirt over his Walk-a-Thon t-shirt—mumbled, "It's complicated," and glanced leerily at me, as he'd been doing since we'd arrived. We sat there in silence and watched them play until she finally announced, "Well, we've got to go to that party, so see ya." They threw backhanded waves at her.

Outside, I asked, "What's this party?"

"It's, you know, a party."

"Yeah, but do we really have to go?"

"What else are we going to do?" she said.

I chuckled awkwardly and didn't push it.

Then we wasted a half hour at Burger King so she could flirt with the pudgy kid working the cash register. His one eye was loose; no lie, he'd be looking at her with his good one and the other one would bob all over the place and creep up toward the ceiling.

"When's your break?" she purred. Leaning, arms crossed on the countertop, casually pushing her breasts together so they spilled slightly out of the rip at the top of her t-shirt. "I drove past your house this afternoon. Did you see me? You were out raking leaves. You didn't see me. That's okay." Hands fluttering around his elbow. "I would've stopped, but I couldn't. I had a . . . I was late for this thing." Some customers came in, and he gave us free Mountain Dews, told us to wait, he'd meet us out back.

I shuffled behind her into the parking lot and tried unsuccessfully to dream up an escapade compelling enough to transform the evening. I was insulted by how things were going; I had it all over each one of these guys, yet she fawned on them as if they were God's gift and left me, in their presence, to lurk dumbly behind her without even an introduction. I was just a prop, a shadowy figure from a different world, trotted out to show the boys how desirable she was. Or—and I preferred to see it this way—I was the one she was trying to impress and make jealous. Keeping this in mind, I could observe her behavior with wry detachment, a condescending tolerance, secure in my own desirability, though I could not hide what I thought of the competition.

"Hey, what's with that guy's eye?"

"Leave him alone."

"I'm just curious. Is he . . . I mean, can he see out of it?"

"He's a sweet guy. I've known him since kindergarten."

"So what happened to his eye?"

"It's just like that."

"Touchy. You like him or something?"

She popped her jaw and peered out from under lowered eyebrows. "He's okay. I let him fuck me if that's what you're asking."

Which, of course, it was, though being told this information so matter-of-factly left me feeling cheated, duped, more by myself than her, like you feel when a con artist convinces you to empty your bank account and willingly hand over every cent, and you realize what kind of person that makes you and what kind of person it makes the con artist. I hid my shock behind what I hoped looked like earnest, empathetic curiosity. My arms hung limp and conspicuous at my sides.

"You sound so bitter when you say that. Did you enjoy it, at least?"

She shrugged. "It was over quick."

She toyed with the skintight bracelet around her wrist as if she were bored, but when she couldn't separate the intertwined strands of plastic, rage suddenly jittered through her body. She ripped the bracelet from her arm, threw it to the blacktop, and ground it into the tarmac with the platform sole of her sneaker.

I found myself actually caring about her. "So why do you hang out with him?"

"Who, Stevie? He's got the best weed in town, okay?"

Stevie got us stoned behind the green dumpster. I braced myself against it with a stiff arm and watched them chatter while considering what I'd just learned about their relationship. He was the silent type, but she made up for this with stream-of-consciousness riffs, paraphrased from books she didn't understand, I was sure, about what it means to be "fully alive, really alive, not like the fuck-alls in this town." She touched him incessantly, but I noticed now that he was barely conscious of her attention. His good eye was as unfocused as his bad one; though he gazed vaguely at her, the iris was dilated and he twitched every time the lights of a car trolled past. She kissed him on the cheek as we were leaving. "You're my hero, Stevie. You're going to call me tomorrow?" He shrugged and I doubted that he'd remember she existed by the time he got back to the cash register.

I felt great affection and pity for her now. "What was that all about?" I asked.

She ignored me.

I took a risk. She was a few feet ahead of me, and I reached out and placed my hands on her shoulders, a simultaneously freewheeling and possessive gesture. She didn't brush me off, but she also didn't bend under my weight and invite a chin on the collar or an arm around the waist.

"So," I said, "what's the deal with that Stevie guy?"

"You were there."

"I couldn't follow it. I need a context."

"I'll tell you if you let go of me."

I loosened my grip slightly and she spun and ran giggling to the car.

Instead of chasing after her, I flicked my shoulders like I was stretching, working out a knot. I cracked my neck. I continued slowly, as if I were cool and unrattled, to the driver's-side door, where I pulled my keys from my pocket, spinning the ring on my index finger so they slapped clicking into my palm, and unlocked the doors, all the while staring into her eyes—intensely I thought—trying to force on her the understanding that I was more serious and dangerous than her stoner playmates, that I was humoring her with my time, not vice versa.

"You fail," she said, hopping into the car.

"At what?"

"You just fail." She flicked on the radio and scanned the stations, giving each song half a second, two or three notes, before rejecting it with a grimace or sigh.

"Okay, fine, I fail, but at what?"

"If I have to tell you, you *really* fail." She continued scanning the stations until they began to repeat, and then she flopped in disgust back in her seat.

We idled in the Burger King parking lot listening to power chords, the car still in park, and I wondered if I should start driving. I didn't know where she would take me next, though, and since there were no distractions here, I wanted to find an in while I had the chance.

"Maybe if I knew what I failed at, I could—"

"Don't you have any tapes?"

"Sure. What do you want to listen to?"

"Something good, I don't know. Where are they?"

"First tell me what it is I failed at."

"Forget it. Let's just go."

She found me laborious. I found her tedious—or wanted to. Instead, I was charmed. She was so much better at living than I was.

"You don't like me much, do you?" I said.

"I like you fine. Let's go."

I watched her body language. She was pinched everywhere, curled in an upright fetal position, brow furrowed, lips pursed. I held my gaze in the hope she would return it, that I would receive at least this small kindness, a moment of eye-to-eye contact, possibly a sneaking smile to let me know that, despite appearances, she still thought we might have something in common. She held out. Her cheek pulsed with tension. Giving up, I released the parking brake. Then I reached over her and popped open the glove compartment. She yielded as my arm brushed her calf, spreading her legs to make room while I fished around for a tape.

"Is Lapin okay? He's all I've got."

She sighed. "Fine," and as soon as I was out of her way, she snapped her legs shut.

We listened to my friend Lapin Milk's demo as I squealed the tires in frustration and defeat, and spun out into the street. Lapin's folk-tinged rock and roll, so earnest, tormented and lyrically loopy, so in love with the pain of love, eased us out of our separate selves. Neither of us could help but to mumble along to the morbid chorus: *You hit and you run / You tore me to shreds / You left me mangled / You left me for dead / You bailed with the best parts of me.* The windows were open, and the backdraft whipped and swirled through the car. All the way across town, I gauged the intonations of her shifting posture, watching her tension and annoyance flutter away like loose parking tickets in the circulating air. Eventually her shoulders slumped, her feet fell to the floor. Legs splayed, calves crossed, she slipped off her sandals and wiggled her toes, and I began to feel emboldened. While shifting gears, I allowed myself to brush her outer thigh, lightly, subtly, lingering just for a second, as if by coincidence.

She sat up. "Hey, how *is* Lapin?"

I'd been fearing this question all night. Lapin Milk, formerly Nate Parker, was a big deal, the only kid making the rounds of the podunk local clubs who had more talent than ego. He'd just returned from Boston, where he'd been going to some fancy music school for the past year. The people there—self-important, pretentious, the worst kind of music geeks—just didn't get it, so fuck them, he came home before they could embitter him and destroy his passion. Unlike them, he really had something to say, and chose to protect what he knew over making the contacts and capitalizing on the buzz the school offered. He didn't care about fame, but about being understood, and anyway, if you're good enough, the industry will come to you. *I* understood him: we'd been friends for years, since we'd been the two worst players on JV baseball, taking up space on the far end of the bench and trying to pinpoint exactly what we found so profound about the piercing metaphysical cry that is Bowie's *Aladdin Sane*.

And she thought *she* understood him, though in fact, the way Lapin told it, she pestered him, annoyed the shit out of him, calling him four, five, ten times a day until finally he got a caller ID box and began answering only when he had another girl over. She willfully misunderstood—or maybe got off on—his sadistic and ruthless exegeses on how this or that girl, whoever he had there, was such a better fuck than she was. "She's crazy," he told me. "She's obsessed. She won't take a hint."

"Lapin's fine," I said. "He's, you know, keeping on."

She lit a cigarette, still casual, and blew the smoke out the window. "I haven't talked to him in forever. He's . . . Is he pissed at me or something?"

"No, I don't know. He's . . . you'd have to ask him."

"He must've said something."

I fumbled for a cigarette of my own, a sympathy cigarette. I couldn't tell her what Lapin thought of her. For one thing, I didn't want to believe he was right. Sure, when I'd met her at his gig, she'd kept an eye on him, watching him as he slid back and forth across the bar buying Kamikaze after Kamikaze for his hangers-on, but unlike his other girls, she'd actually seemed sort of interested in me. For another thing, if his assessment was true, I didn't want to know about it. And raising the topic could only lower my odds. I'd become the go-between, the neuter, the friend—no longer a sexual threat.

I'd fallen for her that night. She was so bold. She strutted instead of swishing. When we played pool, she gripped her stick like she had a table in her basement, lined up her shots, made them. During my turns, she swung herself around the room as if she was beyond pining for charming princes and knew how to handle boozy Don Juans, like if someone touched her, it would be because she'd decided he could; she'd make the calls and name the positions. In the middle of our game, some paunchy old fuck woozed up and hulked over her, slobbering something into her ear, his eyes glassy, his whole body swooning. Instead of freaking out, she chuckled. "Any way you want it, baby," she said as she slapped her own ass. That was all it took to shake him off. Here is a girl, I'd thought, who's all outward rush, so well defended from sentiment and introspection that she's impervious to the long-term damage they, like chemical weapons, wreak on the rest of us. What finally cinched my desire was how, when I probed for her fragile secrets, asking why she was so angry, she laughed in my face and said, "What? You think you're some kind of shrink or something? I'm not angry." I raised a single incredulous eyebrow. "But you are . . . It's just . . . it's all over you. You're all aggression. How come?" Without answering, as if my question were meaningless, she swiveled her stool, turning her back on me, and entered the heated debate about vegetarianism taking place among the girls seated on her other side. I knew then that she was protecting something unfathomably precious, and the fact that I couldn't stride past her defenses, I was sure, intimated that, when I finally managed to tip-toe into the chamber where she kept her riches, I would discover the someone I was so desperate to love.

"Listen, Lapin's . . . he's kind of a sort of rock star, you know?"

"So?"

"He just, he has different ways of . . . He's different than we are."

"How would you know?"

"We're best friends."

"Well, fine, okay. But you don't even *know* me."

I couldn't help wincing when I heard her say this.

"You don't know how I am."

"I've been paying attention."

She squirmed, skeptical, but for the first time, curious, suscep-tible to my wiles. "Oh? So, like, what do I do?"

I could say . . . what? I could say that, while Lapin did whatever he wanted, secure as he was in his sustained blessedness, in his born right to be the constant center of attention, myopically selfish, thus freeing those around him from the burden of his existence, her every action was tactical, an attempt to surprise or shock or seduce, and like me she didn't exist when others weren't there to witness her. While I suspected this was correct, it was maybe too aggressive. She'd bristle and lose interest. It was a quip when I needed a koan. I could cut deeply, let her know I was on to her, that I saw how everything she'd done tonight—from accepting my com-pany simply because I was Lapin's friend to breaking in on the poker game and showing me off at Burger King—was tied together by her insecurity, by her gargantuan capacity for self-loathing. I could say anything, and if I was vague enough and included plenty of caveats and loopholes, it would ring true. But I didn't want to manipulate her. I wanted, actually, to understand her—and though I knew she'd scoff at the very thought—to *be there* with her.

"I don't know," I said after numerous deep, contemplative drags on my cigarette. "Do you actually want to talk about this?"

"Sure."

"We'll have to pull over somewhere."

"We're almost at the party."

"We can't talk about this at the party."

"Sure we can."

"You'll have to play with your friends."

"No." That dumbfounded, judgmental expression. "There it is. Turn. Turn."

"Which—where?"

She tapped my shoulder like it was a conga and reached across in front of me.

"Left, right there."

The party—I use the term loosely—consisted of a mob of teenagers crammed into the parking lot of a landscaped municipal park. They all looked alike: blond, crisp t-shirts embossed with tableaus of surfboards and sunglasses and fun in the sun, tucked into freshly ironed blue jeans. The boys all wore brand-new basketball shoes; the girls, Tretorns. The same swarm of people who, under different names, spread like a virus through my town, and whom I'd fled tonight to try my luck with her. As I trolled through the parking lot, swerving around them, I gripped the wheel tensely and wished one of them would slip a foot under my tire, just by mistake, so I could randomly crush it and pull the world crashing down around him. She, meanwhile, flipped down the visor and checked herself in the mirror, fidgeting with her barrettes, rubbing a wet finger at the edges of her eyes, turning and peering, angling for a side view of herself. We were being sized up, a thousand petty questions asked and answered in a glance, and if they'd failed my test, I was failing their test as well. So was she. The boys were smirking, the girls were whispering. One guy held his fingers to his mouth in a **V** and rapidly flicked his tongue through the slit. We weren't wanted here, and I couldn't believe she didn't already know this.

I parked in the darkness away from the crowd. "So these are your friends, huh?"

"These are my friends. Yes." Her speech was clipped now. She sat back, away from me. Her eyes seemed to dare me to disagree.

But why put myself through her justifications? I couldn't be more disappointed than I already was. Suddenly she wasn't so mysterious or surprising, just an empty, insecure girl nakedly desiring a society that didn't want her. I could see now why she put up with Lapin's sadism—at least it was one-on-one. With these people she was the knowing butt of a sophomoric joke.

"You really think we'll be able to talk here?"

"Chill out, man."

"No, it's alright with me—you're the one who wanted to talk. I just . . . this isn't really my scene."

"You want to go? Fine. Fine. We can go. What do you want to do? Get an ice cream cone and hold my hand? No, you want to go park somewhere so you can beg me for a blow job, don't you? That's cool. How about here? Whip it out. Let's have at it."

I felt myself leaving. Saw myself driving the back roads home, blasting the college radio station where maybe I'd find some punk rock and reporting all this tomorrow to Lapin who'd laugh and say, "You should've at least fucked her."

"Look, I could . . . it's—what?—*late* . . . I could go home. Why don't I just leave you off here and you can catch a ride from somebody."

"I'm sorry," she said, with contrition I knew was meant to manipulate. "I didn't mean that."

"No?"

"No. I . . . I wanted to see what you'd do."

"Well, now you know. I'm not as base as you think. And listen, believe it or not, and I know you don't want to, but we don't all think with our dicks."

"I never said that."

"But that's what you think, no?"

She looked like she was about to cry.

"Isn't it?"

"No."

She slid over and balanced next to me on the edge of the driver's seat. Twisting to keep from falling, she snuck her arms around my waist and pressed her face into my chest. I felt bad about myself, I don't know why.

"Hey," I said. "Hey, look at me for a second, okay?" Her cheeks were dry and smooth. I cupped her chin in my two hands. "Some people have good intentions."

I felt like a sham, even as I said it, but whereas earlier I'd had every intention of trying to seduce her—to be like the others but with, I imagined, more class, more delicacy—I now really did want my good intentions to prevail over my wet dreams. Then again, I wondered if, here, in my arms, she was maybe less safe than she'd been with any man to whom she'd previously bartered her body for attention. I would happily forestall sex for the possibility of a more elusive intimacy. I was dangerous to her exactly because I wasn't going to make a play. I posed no physical threat, but I suspected the stern kindness I was displaying was more disruptive to her sense of self than the aggressive thrust she had come to expect from boys brandishing their dicks like knives. I posed an ontological threat. She knew what to do with a hard-on, that was easy, but a man? Maybe not.

I flattered myself like this as she leaned in and kissed me, her lips probing for pliancy, her teeth scraping at the edges of my mouth, her tongue prying at my teeth.

I refused to give in.

"Why are you doing this?" I asked.

"I don't know. It seemed like the right thing."

"Well, stop."

"You don't like it?"

"It doesn't matter if I like it, it's not"—I searched for the word—"genuine. Why don't you wait and kiss me when you mean it?"

"Does that mean you're going to stay?"

"And if you're not capable of being genuine, then don't kiss me at all."

"But you're going to stay?"

"For how long?"

"An hour, maybe?"

I made a point of checking my watch—11:24.

"Okay, an hour."

Sullen, I sat on a picnic table at the farthest edge of the pale circles of light illuminating the parking lot and watched her pretend that she was the same breed as these other girls. It was as if the kids at the party had held up a picture of a girl—a sweet young thing, a girl next door—who looked nothing like her and said, "If this were you we'd accept you," and in taking this impossible challenge, she'd succeeded in partially sublimating her most unique and charming features—her explosive, devouring anger, the speed with which she twirled chaos around in her hand, her sexualization of everything—but failed miserably at taking on the bouncy, smiley duplicity, the faux naïveté, of the girl in the picture. Flitting from the edge of one group to another, she was a parody of everything they stood for. Her false smile glaringly false, almost but not quite ironic, while theirs—smiling because that was what you were supposed to do—seemed simply stupid. Her posture loose-limbed and flexible despite her efforts to repress everything her body knew. Her absurd attempts to thrust herself into their conversations. Two girls compare notes: "I'm so drunk." "I *know*. Me too." "We should slow down, maybe." And her attempt at a joke, "You won't get laid that way." They scowl, they hiss. Does she realize she's the aggressive one, I wonder, even here where she's trying to be meek? The performance would've been hilarious if she'd known that she was mocking them, that they were the laughable ones. Instead, it was pathetic. Dejected, she slunk away from the girls.

The boys at the party were even less subtle, twisting her nipples, flipping their fingers up between her legs. It wasn't even heartbreaking. She turned her head to the sky and laughed. "You wish you could have a piece of this." But that didn't stop them. "That dripping thing? My dick would fall off." Or, "Only if you did all three of us at once." When no one would give her a beer, she begged. One of them finally said, "I've got some beer for you," and with crude bravado, he began unzipping his fly. He stopped when he got the laugh he was after, but she wasn't resisting. She was whatever they wanted her to be. So little self-respect. The irony was that she thought that they, everyone there in that parking lot, were the intimidating ones, when in fact, she scared them to death, and through her example of what *not* to do, got the girls to pray for their own chastity and kept the boys awake late into the night rubbing away their memories of her cleavage. All they knew of her was sex, and despite herself, that's all she presented to them. Hardly immune to this, I found myself asking: Who is she here to ensnare tonight? How many of these boys have had her on nights when they knew there was no one around to see?

Not that I cared, really, not anymore. I no longer wondered how Lapin could miss the sweet sadness and beauty I saw in her. It wasn't there. I had imagined it. Now that I knew this, what more was there for me to learn about her? Oh, so much more than I needed to, because when the cops came and scattered the party, she found me and dragged me deep into the park where we hid behind a shrub and, while waiting for them to leave, finally had that long conversation.

I guess I'll admit that by now she had become an object, an icon, albeit defaced and desecrated, of a certain kind of fertility: the whorish, skanky kind. Having assimilated the opinions of all of the friends she'd subjected me to tonight, I wanted to fuck her quick, speed home and shower. So, call me a prick. Call me an asshole. Tell me I'm as bad as she is. I won't disagree, but I will say that my intent had been kind at the start, it's just that, after wasting four hours as the only man — or woman, for that matter, or boy or girl — so desperate and self-deluded as to believe she was worth his kindness, I'd grown tired of trying to defy her expectations. She'd broken me down. Which is why, as we lay side by side on our stomachs, peering through the tangled lower brambles of the hedgerow at the distant flashlights and headlights and red-and-blue twirling lights atop the cop cars, wondering how long before they receded and freed us from hiding, I dug my leg under hers and flipped over, yanking her toward me like the other half of a bear trap. I palmed the cheeks of her ass and rippled my fingers, kneading the baby fat. I felt for resistance. I grappled with my own shock at myself. I took her body into my arms—reached out and grabbed—without even asking myself what she might want. And I wondered how this aggressive new me could have wasted so much time dodging the truth, cloaking his billy-goat self in the soft kid gloves of a gentleman's skittishness, the monk's itchy hair shirt of moral hesitation. Rolling us over so I was on top, I roughly kissed her. It was so easy. What a relief: I wasn't the nice guy I'd thought I was. I was capable of being like all the rest.

"Hey." She was unfazed. Unimpressed. "What do you think you're doing?"

"Nothing."

"You're not doing nothing. You're trying to fuck me."

"No, I'm not. I'm just . . . messing around."

I pushed up her t-shirt and, wedging my fingers under her lacy black bra, I pulled a breast loose and ran my thumb over the aureole. Her nipple was unaroused. Massaging, sucking, nipping did no good; the skin would crinkle, the nub would rise, but only momentarily, intermittently, with resignation. Mere physiology. I didn't capture her imagination. She lay there silently, arms at her sides. I placed my ear to her nipple and gazed at her face, which likewise betrayed no emotion.

"What's the matter?" I asked her.

"Nothing. Are you done?"

"I don't know. You don't seem to be liking this."

"It's fine."

"Really?"

"No, but . . . whatever. Hey, did Lapin tell you I'd let you fuck me just cause you're his friend or something?"

"Uh . . . no."

"Cause I'm sort of seeing him, you know."

"Okay."

She propped herself up on her elbows to look at me. "Okay? Is that a yes-I-know okay? Or a no-I-didn't-know-and-since-you're-seeing-my-best-friend-I'll-get-off-of-you-and-let-you-put-your-tit-away okay?"

"I guess a yes-I-know okay."

"Oh. Alright."

She lay back down, but what could I do? I kissed her shoulder and asked, "Are you in love with him?"

"No, I'm obsessed. There's a difference."

"Tell me about it."

"You really don't want to know."

"Sure I do."

"It's complicated," she said, but I got her to tell me. I didn't know that it meant hearing her whole life story.

Her father, that night when he entered her room, stopped and swayed every few feet, staggering from doorway to dresser to desk to bed. He sat on nothing and then sat again, with a jolt, on the mattress, lunging to keep himself from toppling. He shoved a heavy palm into her inner thigh. "Ow, Daddy, that hurts." He leaned over her. His body, built like a beer keg, was crushing her. "Don't— what do you want?" Saliva hung like stalactites from the dark cave of his mouth, falling loose, twirling, cold, down onto her cheek. "You know damn well what I want." She was pretty sure this was true, just as she'd known what his brother had wanted that afternoon, but she said, "No, I don't. Daddy, you're drunk, you're scaring me, what do you want?" because she didn't want to believe this of her own father. "I want to know who you've been fucking." Whoa—not what she expected. "Nobody," she said. "Don't lie to me." "It's true." That's when he slapped her. "I said don't lie to me.

You don't get to be a whore without fucking anybody." These were
his words, as if being a whore was something for which only the
fearless were chosen, yet also, because of his tone, as if being a
whore meant that she was untethered from him, that she belonged
to no one now and was thus everyone's property. "Really, Dad,
nobody. You woke me up." He pulled away from her. The night
was muggy and all she had on was a t-shirt—one of his—and cotton undies with one tiny flower sewn onto the waistband. He sized
her up; the sheet between them hid nothing. Was that a lascivious
look in his eyes? She couldn't tell. They were glassy, rheumy. "If I
ever catch you . . . I'll kill you. I'll rip your heart out and feed it to
him, whoever the fucker is." This threat was not quite idle: as he
shuffled out of the room, she felt like he *had* ripped her heart out—
but who could he feed it to? Her sin this day had had no accom-
plice. Her carnal knowledge was entirely hypothetical.

   Good riddance, she would eventually say, but first she had to
learn the wiles by which she would live from now on. The next
morning her mother wouldn't come near her, didn't ask for help
with the dishes or the garden or any of the housewife chores she'd
previously been teaching piecemeal to her daughter. Instead, her
mother gave her these cockeyed looks that said, What has become
of you? I'm disappointed, I disapprove, so whatever you do with
your life, don't blame me.

   From then on she did what she wanted. If she was sullied
already, she might as well play in the mud. She messed around
with whoever, did whatever felt right in the moment. She put out,
so what? Everyone knew she was that kind of girl, why deny it?
When her uncle came around, drunk again, looking for action, she
gave it to him, repeatedly. They had a thing for a while. Her father
knew, he must have. They'd flirt in front of him. They'd go for
walks from which they'd return blushing, not touching, smirking
and straightening their clothes and hair and lying that they'd been
bird-watching. They fucked in her parents' bed once while they
were at a Friday fish fry. Her father didn't care though, not really.

After that one night, he'd given up on her. Or maybe, unable to bear their abhorrent behavior, he convinced himself that his suspicions sprang from his paranoid mind. Or maybe he realized that if he were his brother and this tart were his niece instead of his daughter, well, maybe then he'd be the one tasting young flesh. He could judge and distance himself from the crime, but he could not condemn it. For whatever reason, he let these things happen. Her mother remained on the margins, where she'd always been. Never one to assert anything too loudly, she did what she'd done all her life: sit in the background and watch, brokenhearted. The whole family, it seemed, had fallen from grace.

She sensed that was what they felt, but she saw things differently. Her beliefs, as she expressed them to me, were vehemently self-forgiving, defiant, defensive, fanatical, so much more self-assured than her behavior all evening had shown her to be. Simply put, she thought you're either a prude, trapped in your too-tight white dress, or you're a whore, free to swing in the zoom of the world. At some point in their lives, everyone must choose one way or the other. And it's a pity, but still it's true, that the prudes, those tight-asses who don't know what they're missing, they're the ones who decide what's right and what's wrong. Which doesn't mean they're not all whores behind closed doors. It's just that they've mastered duplicity, and of course—duh—why wouldn't they despise the people like her who call them on their bullshit? Really we're all whores, but only a few of us—those willing to combust in public view—can accept the fact and get on with it. She was, she claimed, a martyr to the truth. "And the truth is that life is all zoom, all speed and forward thrust. If you stop and look for the goodness, life races forward and leaves you to die."

I wasn't sure how I felt about this. I'm not even sure she believed it. But as I said, it ruined the mood. Though I had tried to be a brutal man, I was, at heart, soft and scared, inclined toward looking for goodness in myself if not necessarily the world. "Did you come up with that all by yourself?"

"Basically. Yeah."

"You don't think anybody else sort of helped put those ideas in your head? Not even a little bit?"

"You think I'm stupid, don't you."

"I didn't say that."

She heaved an arch sigh.

"Alright," I said, trying to save myself. "So what does all that have to do with obsession? What about Lapin?"

Her answer took so long to come that I thought she was done with me, that she'd decided to lie there and stare up at the sky and think her thoughts and wait until I went away.

When she did speak, it was as if she were holding her emotions apart so the words could slip out like ghosts. "Lapin's like me. He's . . . we're the same. Except when he does it, it makes him sexier. Everyone loves him for it. They . . . forgive him or something. I don't know. And . . ."

I couldn't see her face. I thought she might be crying, but I didn't move to look.

"I feel . . . normal with him. I want to be with him. All the time. It's like, if I was, there'd be nothing wrong with me."

I didn't know what to do. My fingers were twined under my chin, my palms flat on her rib cage. Her spread legs cradled my body, casually, almost but not quite incidentally. I was aware of the size and shape of every touch: her thighs yielding to my hipbones; her pelvis nestling up to my navel and swaddled in two different fabrics, the sheer poly-synth of her miniskirt and the absorbent cotton beneath it; the slight feather brush of an ankle against my knee; and, most disconcertingly, her exposed stomach, the unsteady rhythm of her breath coming and going, caressing my sternum and then withdrawing. A deep inhalation would press her abdomen into my chest and raise me an inch or two. Her breasts would shimmy like jello. Her awareness of our two bodies seemed heightened as well. She didn't swat at the fly that crawled along her shoulder. She twitched her nose instead of scratching. When she did move, it was with a delayed reaction, as if she were thinking: *My scalp itches and there's my arm on the grass, my thumb an inch from his elbow, so I'll lift it and quickly scratch the itch; there, that's okay, now, I'll put my arm back exactly where it was, but no, slightly closer, so my thumb touches his elbow.* Despite all this physical intimacy, despite what my body was telling me, I didn't want her, it seemed wrong to want her, and who knows what she wanted, she definitely didn't want me.

"It was the same with my uncle. Except more fucked-up."

I wondered which was more compassionate: to continue holding her, sublimating my own rage, and trying to comfort her for pains that she claimed didn't hurt, or to pull away and go home where I could be safe from the sordid life to which she was committed.

"Anyway," she said, "listen, I need some drugs or a drink or some something. Then I should drag my sorry ass home. Do I have to let you fuck me to get a ride?"

I didn't have the heart to say no. It would've disappointed her, pissed her off, I think. I don't know. Maybe she wouldn't have cared either way. At the time, though, I thought I was being kind.

When we got to her house, I leaned over to kiss her on the cheek. I didn't want to, but it seemed like the chivalrous thing to do. She pulled away, the expression on her face disgusted, scornful.

Her name was Emmy; it seems important in retrospect. I didn't see her again after that. I think Lapin saw her a few times, but I can't be sure, I never asked him directly. I couldn't. I didn't want to know.

I was eighteen, and before her I'd only slept with one girl, with whom sex had been about love, about romance. It's not anymore. Emmy was right. Like everyone else, I have failed.

Sobieski, BG

u32.3691148

Her life will be spent strapped in strollers, in high chairs, alone in the cluttered living room, and on the rare occasions when she is toted out of the house, she'll be shackled to a plastic saddle in the back seat of the car, locked all afternoon behind cracked windows in a parking lot or, rarely, placed on a chair that hangs in the air and pushed back and forth until she is dizzy. Her mother and father will leave her for hours in a plastic cage full of toys in the living room while they do the things that adults do—things she'll never fathom; she'll never be old enough to do adult things too. All she will know is that her parents usually aren't in the room with her, that they are elsewhere, that she is alone. Sometimes she'll hear noises from other rooms and she'll recognize them as the sounds of her parents, but they'll be muffled and there won't be anything else—not even shadows wavering behind the open doors—to intimate that other people are actually nearby. Her closest friends will be the flat cutouts of animals—a tiger, a bear, a donkey and two kangaroos—dangling from the ceiling, spinning inches out of reach. One day, full of excitement, her father will bring home a box made of plastic and glass and arrange it on a low ledge in the living room. Her mother will point a small black object at the box, and the glass will brighten with color—rooms opening up inside the box and people sitting inside these rooms. The girl will lie on the floor watching these people. She'll be able to see and hear them, and they will become her friends, though she'll know they are not like her. One morning her mother will brighten the box very early. In the glass, the girl will see smooth round heads and small faces with bright bulging cheeks. She'll see spit-dappled lips, tiny pug noses, glazed and stopped-up nostrils, eyes popped wide open with wonder and joy. For the first time she'll see people who are small, like her. Babies. She'll stop chewing and drop her red plastic doughnut. Every day she'll watch the children playing with one another and wish that she could play too. Her infantile image of life will stretch to accommodate other small people convening in sunlight to do nothing but be together. She'll gurgle and point and crawl toward the babies, intent on joining them, touching them, laughing and cooing and toddling with them. She'll pull herself up until she is standing. She'll hug the warm glowing box. As it topples off of the ledge she will totter and then collapse under its weight, believing that the children are rushing toward her, extending their love.

Have you ever gone to Love's Drugstore and asked for razor blades, the ones that cut on two sides? I have, Dad. I did it again today.

What did you think about on the walk home? Did you think about me? Or Mom? I bet you thought about Mom. I bet some memory from back when the two of you were an inseparable team was lodged in your brain like a tumor. I can imagine the scene: an opening-night party, maybe in the Public's front lobby; she was the ingenue — in life as in art — and you were the man she adored. The hoity patrons, the rest of the cast, the director, the theater's staff, maybe even Joe Papp himself, all made their way to her, gulping down white wine spritzers, munching on satay and salmon pockets. The room worked her. She was boxed in by people who were, for the night, in awe of her, who wanted to be near her, wanted a piece of her they could claim as their own, but who knew from her professionally charming small talk, her broad smile, her gracious, almost disbelieving gratitude when they got around to their awkward, embarrassed praise, that she was still acting. I bet on your way home from Love's, you remembered how she glanced around the room for you during these parties and, once she found you, she momentarily broke character, blushing, eyes twinkling. You would mime pouring wine over the head of the thousand-dollar donor talking at her, and she'd twitch her nose flirtatiously, like a rabbit, before snapping back to work. It was as if the two of you had an inside joke, your irreverence reminding her that these fund-raising events weren't nearly as important as the sustenance you gave her throughout the months and months in between shows, when she felt forgotten, like a failure; it strengthened her, helped her endure the brief, minor, meaningless nights of pretending she actually was a star. As a little girl at those parties, I felt like I was the star, like my parents were the coolest, most in-love people in the world, and when the grown-ups at the parties crouched and asked me about second grade and if I wanted to be an actor or artist like one of you, they saw me not as a little brat out after bedtime but as the incarnation of something exceptional, the extension and twining of each of your talents, the palpable evidence, the public proof of your private love.

As you trudged home from the drugstore, how long did it take for you to begin speculating on what she's up to now? Did you imagine her on location for that period piece, buying sandals at a street stall in Athens—or some man, her director or costar, buying them for her—and wonder what would happen if you flew there to . . . rescue her is what you probably told yourself. I know you got the address of her hotel off the package she sent me, but that won't be much help; she left there three weeks ago and now she's vacationing in Hydra. Even if you found her, what would you say? That you love her? You can't live without her? All that blah, blah, blah? Can you think of anything that would surprise her even a little bit? If you say yes, you're lying. The power dynamics between you two have atrophied. It's like arthritis: the joints don't pivot, the muscles clench in a gnarled tension. She's an actor, Dad, and you were always in too much awe of her. You should throw away all the photos from that show you devoted to her—and the contact sheets, too. Now that she's found sustained adoration from an audience larger than two, she no longer needs you—she needs me, she's still periodically compelled to tell me she loves me, but that's just so she can feel wholesome and less like a fraud when she thinks about what she's achieved in her life. If you were to find her in Europe and confront her, whatever words you used, you'd say only one thing: *Why don't you need me anymore?* And she'd have only one response: *Because I already have you.* Of course you know this without me telling you, but that doesn't help, does it? You still—at least until today you did—obsessively imagine other scenarios . . . but Love's is only a quick hop from our building, not a long enough walk for you to have a thought you haven't had so many times already that even you find it boring.

I understand you, Dad. The shrink you send me to thinks I have an unhealthy identification with you, but I don't, it's just that I'm just like you. This was a big issue right after Mom left, but then, for a while, I was my own person. I credit this to Yegal. Remember him? I told you about him last fall when you and I got stoned in your studio.

He was the assistant art teacher from that summer class I took at the New School. He came up behind me the second week of class and, while explaining how I might expand the emotional breadth of the painting I was working on at the time, he rubbed my back—not with a soft, slight palm on the spine, but with both hands, his thumbs kneading my shoulders—a rub I couldn't misinterpret as mere teacherly encouragement. Even though Yegal was generally touchy-feely with everyone, this was different; the placement and movement of his hands was careful, timid. There was a level of self-consciousness about it that made me nervous. I freaked out. I didn't go back to class. A week later, Yegal showed up during my shift at the Downtown Guggenheim, smiling out the side of his mouth. He leaned against the wall outside the gift shop until I took a break. His hair was matted flat on the left side, and I wanted to comb it for him. I wanted to wash his clothes. Even though, at twenty-two, he was closer to being the adult than I was, I felt like he needed me to take care of him. He couldn't do it himself. I walked especially slow and kept my distance, leaning back defensively and jutting out my jaw at him. He glanced around the lobby and then said, "Hey." "Hey, yourself," I said. "I mean . . . Hi." "Surprise, surprise." "Are you okay?" "Why wouldn't I be?" "You haven't been in class since . . ." "So?" "I, um, I thought maybe I'd . . . okay, it's like this. There's the line, right?" He drew his foot along one of the cracks in the floor. "I thought maybe I'd—" He stepped over the line, toward me. "Like that." And he cracked his halfway smile. That was too sweet already, sticky and sappy, and I tried to resist letting it touch me. I think I might have even scoffed. He'd been hiding one hand behind his leg. "I got you a present." He held out a paper bag. "It's Rilke. Do you know Rilke?" "No. Well, sort of. I've heard of him," I said, not moving to take the bag. "Rilke's great . . . really great." The longer I waited, the more his arm sagged and strained to hold the bag up in front of me. "I picked it up at that used bookstore over on Sixth. Have you been there? It's great. You can actually find what you're looking for." I still didn't take the bag. His arm finally fell, and after shaking out the strain in his muscles, he unsheathed the book and leafed through it. "It's dedicated to some girl named Ruthie. From, um, Ben. And she seems to have marked it up and underlined her favorite parts. So, you, while you read it, you can sort of imagine what their love was like and speculate on what might've happened that was so huge for her to throw the book away. I . . . um . . . I thought you might appreciate that sort of thing. Take a look." I hesitated, but since I knew I was going to take it eventually, I thought, fine, this'll be when. I swiped the book from him and tried to make sure he understood that it was the book, not him, that interested me. I thumbed through it, trying to look bored. "Check this out," he said. "This is my favorite. 'Turning Point.'" I let him stand next to me and flip through the pages as I held the book by the spine. He read the poem out loud to me. It *is* a great poem, and Yegal must've known that I'd listen to it with an ear toward figuring out what he was telling me—that something about me inspired him to "do heart-work," like the man in the

poem is told he must do. I fell for it, Dad. I'm a sucker . . . and
Yegal seemed so pained and honest, so awkward, while he stood
there waiting for my response. I threw my arms around his neck
and let my legs give out so all that held me up was him. I let him
kiss me . . .

But why am I going on like this? I'm obsessing, just like you do.
It's as if I'm trying to paint his portrait over and over again in my
mind, and if I get it perfect, he'll suddenly be here next to me.

I didn't do this before he disappeared to that artists' colony in
Vermont two months ago. When I told you about him before, I was
really only interested in me, in the changes going on in me as I fell
in love. I rambled childishly about the squirrelly feeling I got in my
stomach every time he reached out to touch or kiss me. How safe
and cozy I felt each time he stopped himself—conscious of the
danger involved in flirting with the physical boundaries he'd
placed on his desire—from caressing certain parts of my body. The
look on your face while I talked was the happiest I'd seen you in
months. The tension relaxed in your cheeks. You stroked the button of skin between your eyebrows, and your crow's-feet came out.
You actually focused—for a couple of hours you were listening to
me, instead of off chopping at the brambles of your memories of
Mom. You said he sounded "hip," and that if I felt comfortable
about it, you'd like to meet him, do the old father thing and size
him up, maybe scare him a little, just to make sure he'd think twice
about breaking my heart. It made me giggle and wince, Dad. I said,
You couldn't scare an eleven-year-old, much less a twenty-two-year-
old, that you're too much my pal to wield any real authority. "Well,
then," you said, "what if I took you two starving artists out to a rock
concert. Or we could see a play? How 'bout it? What if I palled
around with you guys some afternoon? We can . . . hang, or whatever the kids call it now." For a moment I almost considered the
prospect, but I could see from the way your face tightened in on
itself that you were gone, returned to your darkness, brooding, I'm
sure, about the thought of setting foot in a theater with everything

that that connotes: Mom's old friends, Mom's old props, two hours trapped on her turf. "No, that's okay," I said softly. "I just wanted to tell you about him."

Now that he's gone I've been flailing, bleary-eyed from my own loss of love, and overidentifying with you again.

You seem different today, though. This morning, you began to work again. For the first time since Mom left, the red light was on over your darkroom door. After hours in there, you came out all wound up, the muscles in your neck and shoulders tense, and you held your head low like you were flexing your brain. You seemed preoccupied with thoughts that gave you energy instead of taking it away. I should be happy for you, but seeing you like this, so busy and vigorous, depressed me. It propelled me into a kind of self-chastisement. I thought, if Dad can recover his sense of direction, shouldn't I be able to, as well? I tried to will myself into happiness, but instead got stuck and dug deeper and deeper into my sad, worthless self.

What was your lowest point, Dad? The first few months after Mom left? A response to the initial shock of her absence? I bet not. You were still speaking twice a week or so. She'd only done the one movie then, that John Sayles thing, and you still thought she was going to come back from L.A. after pilot season. Remember how that first two weeks slowly stretched to a month, then to two months, then three? How many return tickets did she change before she finally told you she was staying out there indefinitely? And then it was just for the work, so she said, though she hadn't landed a show yet. Her stuff was all here. She didn't want a divorce. How many nights did you and I argue about her right to abandon us? You were the one who defended her, reciting her reasons and ignoring your own emotion. The air there, even with the smog, was somehow less oppressive; it was hopeful air in which anything seemed possible. She didn't dread daylight and wasn't sleeping until noon anymore. Unlike New York, where each day was just like the last except harder to live through, with L.A.'s sun and breeze and the hum of the industry, each day erased the last and she was accountable only to her dreams. She didn't feel guilty about eating well and could rollerblade on Santa Monica Beach; she could be whoever she imagined herself to be, no longer trapped in the precedent of bad behavior, the downtown attitude, that, back here, had been both her draw and her downfall. She was happy, you could tell, and you weren't selfish enough to put your own happiness ahead of what was best for her and her work.

It's called masochism, Dad.

Look at what happened to you in the process. You wandered aimlessly through the Village, staring at pigeons and handing out smokes to the homeless. You used to have this passionate arrogance that showed up in everything you did. When you walked down the street with that slouching strut of yours, people thought you were famous and wondered why they didn't recognize you. But when Mom left, you disappeared as well. Your body was still here, but your mind and your wit and your artistic vision were all packed away in her suitcase like t-shirts. You missed deadlines, turned down money jobs, stopped shooting photographs altogether. The world began to underwhelm you, or Mom overwhelmed your world, I'm not sure which, but either way you were no longer engaged with it in any real, vigorous way. You lived to send her things—it didn't matter what—clothes she'd left behind, that mirror she adored so much, Central Park leaves in the fall.

I can remember one night especially. Mom had been gone over a year. She'd just finished the five-week shoot for *Say You Do*, which was already getting enough buzz to put her in the collage of stars on the covers of the summer blockbuster issues of *Entertainment Weekly* and *Us*. Proclaimed a rising star, she was getting her own write-ups in *Vanity Fair* and *Rolling Stone*. Mentions of you or me were carefully omitted from all the publicity, and despite your rationalizations, you were finally beginning to realize what had happened to your life. On the night I'm thinking of, she called, crying, to tell you her lawyers—she had *lawyers* now—had held a conference call demanding that she divorce you. For the good of her career. She'd already cut ten years off her age. Besides the fact that marriage had been seen as unattractive in focus groups, it was those thirty-six years they were most eager to hide. You and I were liabilities—a sixteen-year-old daughter, a seventeen-year-old marriage—the numbers just didn't add up. And they wanted her to ask, what would it cost to keep you quiet? Do you remember your answer, Dad? Of course you do. Nada. You didn't ask for a thing. You interpreted her blubbering histrionics as a confession of love, and the loss of your right to acknowledge your past, the heartbreaking price of stardom. But you didn't fight for that love, and you never conceded the truth: that actors never stop acting. But you knew. Behind what you wanted to hear, you understood and trembled at what was actually being said. This was her choice, and her career and her lawyers were simply the easiest excuse.

Listening in on the other extension—hearing her lie and you simper, both of you acting like children—I felt it was my duty to be the adult. Or maybe I just wanted to cause a scene, to hurl my anger in both of your faces. I told her she was full of shit, that her story had so many holes that it might as well be made of lace. Didn't she know that the first rule of lying is to keep it simple, and the second to make sure it's plausible? "Be straight with us," I told her. "Show some respect." If you were a sap who was willing to take her bullshit—I was attacking you, too—that's all the more reason for her to be honest. Didn't she know that with love comes the responsibility to have the courage to end it when you know it's over, to make sure you don't engender false hope, to allow the brokenhearted to begin getting over it as quickly as possible? She held to her story, still does, and maybe it really is true—I've heard of nastier things happening out there—but did you notice how quickly her tears stopped after I questioned her script? I was young and livid and I wanted everything to be stark and clear. If the truth was as cruel as I believed it was, I wanted the cruelty to be explicit, so we could all see what we'd stepped in. How was I supposed to have known that, even though this was the end of our family, you and I would still cling to what-ifs and how-comes?

And why didn't you reprimand me once we'd all hung up? Was it because this was the night that you walked down to Love's and bought razor blades? Was the pain so fierce that killing it overwhelmed all other concerns?

Or did you know I just wouldn't listen, that I'd race off to the Continental to flirt with my own self-destructive impulses before you had the chance to say anything? Maybe knowing this released you, in your mind, from responsibility. I understand, Dad. I can imagine how abstract everything else must've seemed that night.

What did you do with the blades, though, when you got home? Did you set the little yellow box out on the table by the window so you could feel their presence as you drank your whiskey and smoked one more joint and, for the last time, watched the she-males work Hudson Street? Did it calm you down just to have them within view? Maybe you did what I do: I lie on the floor of my bedroom with the door locked and the light off, staring at the glow-in-the-dark stars you stuck to the ceiling back when I was little, then I light a few candles and arrange them in a half circle around my head so I can watch the wax pool and drip for a while. It takes some time before I'm ready to open the box and take out a blade. How long did it take you, Dad? Or didn't you get that far? Did you chicken out, throw them down the incinerator shaft in horror and get drunk instead? You did, didn't you? That's okay, everyone does that the first time.

I did go to the Continental that night, but they were carding, and by the time I got there, I didn't really want to be anywhere anymore. I did what you do. I meandered around downtown, picking random destinations just so I'd have a direction to walk in, hoping that, maybe, I'd be ready to let myself be distracted by the time I arrived. First I headed for the Angelika, but halfway there I realized I couldn't stomach sitting through a movie, movies and Mom being synonymous. I imagined myself sitting romantically alone at a corner table at Le Figaro, sipping cappuccino and writing my tortured thoughts down in bad verse on my napkin, looking like a fool, a tourist, and it made me want to throw up. Finally, I pushed through the metal bars closing off Washington Square Park and sat on a bench in the dark. "What about me?" I kept asking myself. "Who's going to take care of me? Who's going to love me?" I don't know how long I sat there. It felt like a second, but must've been at least an hour. It was like I'd floated away. All that existed was me and my sad, massive loneliness. On the walk home, it occurred to me, Fuck it, why not get it over with and float away entirely. I stopped in at Love's and bought razor blades—an impulse buy. But just like you, I didn't use them this first time. I scratched lightly at my wrists, barely drawing blood, then panicked and threw them away.

Even though I was in the midst of falling in love with Yegal, I almost bought a second box while Mom was in town to publicize *Say You Do*. I probably shouldn't tell you that; she left a message on my cell and told me not to say anything. I was going to tell you anyway because I was sure you'd heard she was in town; but the more I thought about it, the more I realized you'd be tortured all week regardless of what I did. You wouldn't sleep, just sit at your post by the window and watch the whores hopping in and out of cars, all the while hoping she'd disregard her worries about what might appear on Page Six, that you'd hear her feet shuffling in the hallway, keys rattling outside the door, and the door would swing open to reveal her, disheveled and distressed and needing you. The two of you would wander down to the Ear—your old haunt—for a drink and a couple hours of wistful remembrance of what it feels like to have soft, pliable hearts, a couple hours of memorizing each other's faces all over again, this time with tears in your eyes. The more I thought about what you'd be going through, the more I realized that telling you she'd made contact with me would be sadistic and cruel. Mom doesn't act on her feelings anymore, doesn't let them show in front of her public (which now includes everyone except her agent, publicist and makeup artist); instead, she hides in hotel rooms until the feelings pass and she can walk, sealed off, iconic and correct, into the glare and assault of the visible world. She would never appear unannounced at our door, disheveled and needy, since the only need she's willing to succumb to is the need for an audience. It's not that the rest of her needs don't exist, it's just that they've been locked away for later, after her wrinkles and sags can no longer be hidden and her career sputters and falters and dies. I wanted to protect you from her. If I'd told you we were meeting, it would only have been a matter of days before you started pressing me for the details.

Seeing her was horrible, Dad. We sat on a bench in the part of Riverside Park that goes over the street—right around Eighty-sixth, I think—with that flower garden. She was explaining how her time is budgeted down to the minute when she's on the publicity junket like this. And when she's not, when she's on the set, it's hours and hours of absolute boredom. There's only so much time one can spend learning lines. She gets cranky and the old feistiness begins bouncing around in her stomach, preparing to burst out at directors and costume designers and bust up her hard-won, easy-to-work-with, nice-girl rep. She asked me to come out and join her in L.A. I could be her personal assistant, since she needs one anyway. It would be fun and the work would be easy, basically just keeping her company, making appointments, keeping track of little details like telling the caterers what she won't eat, balancing her bank book, getting her coffee. Can you believe it? "The best thing," she said, "is we could be together without anybody knowing how old I am." I laid into her. "Is this for real?" I screamed. "Are you really saying this? Why do you think I'd want to give up my whole life— I've got one, too, Mom, and it's not so bad anymore—just to move out to L.A. and be your baby-sitter—not even your fucking daughter, your baby-sitter! I'll stick with Dad, he at least *likes* me. Do you realize we've been here forty-five minutes now and you haven't asked a single thing about me, not even something asinine like what I'm going to do next year after I graduate? And maybe you were going to, but it's too late now. If you do it'll just be because I called you on it." I laid it all out. "Mom, I don't like you and I don't respect you and I'm only here today because you're my mother and I feel like I don't have a choice." The dumpy Upper West Siders—probably the only New Yorkers alive who wouldn't recognize her—made a big show out of giving us space, leering as if we had no right to be in their book-chatty little flower garden, using up their refined air with our trashy, messy lives. Mom's a real pro, now, though. She acted like I was some crazy person who'd randomly chosen her to rant at, and instead of engaging me, she did the dignified thing: she waited for me to stop screaming. Once I'd exhausted myself, she smiled sickly-sweet and said, "It was only a thought."

That's when I stormed off to buy razor blades, but at the last minute I called Yegal instead. He took me out to Veselka for cold borscht. We sat in the back and I stabbed at the purple hard-boiled egg with my spoon. The egg spun and slipped, bobbed in the beet broth, bounced against the plastic edge of the bowl. Yegal ate slowly and watched me. I knew he was watching, and part of what I was doing was manipulative—playing the sullen teenager, dour and sour and dwelling on indescribable troubles, in order to make him feel helpless, to see if he'd get angry and frustrated, or earnestly pressure me to "open up," or treat me like a child, or what. He did the perfect thing, though. Every time I glanced over, he'd say something innocuous. "You know, a beet is a tuber. How does that make you feel?" or "Okay, I was out at Coney Island last weekend, right, and did you know the old Puerto Rican guys who fish on the pier out there use spark plugs as sinkers? It struck me as somehow, I don't know, *real*." or "Stick out your tongue . . . see, it's bright purple. Mine, too. That's the best part. It's like when you're eight years old eating Now and Laters." He kept saying silly things like this until he got me to smirk a little. Eventually, I felt so comfortable that I started babbling about what had happened with Mom. I showed him the faint scratches from the last time I'd bought razor blades. I went on and on about how much I hate her. I'd never told him who Mom was because I'd been afraid his demeanor would change when he found out, but he just listened, cool, unsurprised. He was so sympathetic. Not what I'd expected. I think I subconsciously believed that, by virtue of her fame, Mom was more justified in her negligence than I was in my anger; as if there was something horribly inappropriate, disgraceful even, about my rage when really—her being the star she was—I should be thankful she had time for me at all. But Yegal saw my side, and for the first time I thought, Wait a minute, I'm not the fucking problem, I don't *deserve* this shit. He let me go on for probably forty-five minutes before he pointed at his empty bowl and said, "Soup is good food. Eat up." I laughed and laughed and laughed. I couldn't stop. "Who—" I tried to speak, but speaking made me gag. "Who—" I held up a finger and gulped for air. "Who do—" I doubled over and clutched my stomach—"you think you are—" Holding back laughter made me wheeze. "My mother?" He smirked out the side of his mouth. "No, just her understudy. Come on, let's go look at the river. It's cathartic." He was absurd and perfect and he even paid.

We walked down Ninth, dodged cars across the FDR and climbed the concrete barricade into East River Park. I wrapped my arm around his waist. He rested his on my shoulder, and every few minutes he played with my short jagged hair. He told me how sometimes he forgets he's on an island surrounded by water, and feels trapped and isolated from everything he really cares about— solitude, space, the shapes of the natural world—by the bustle of so many people striving to keep up with their own ambitions. Sometimes he just needs to get near the water, to let his thoughts dissolve into something bigger and more meaningful than a roomful of career-obsessed hipsters. If he were to kill himself, he said, this is how he'd do it: he'd step out into the river, open his mouth and let his lungs fill to overflowing. We watched the tugboats pull barges out toward Staten Island. We watched the traffic speed back and forth across the Williamsburg Bridge. We talked in brief snippets that swirled skyward almost as soon as they entered the air, spun over the retaining wall and fell into the river, mixing with debris and oil as they followed the current downstream. Mom didn't come up once, she wasn't important enough for us to waste our breath on. I felt slightly clichéd, but that was just my cynical resistance to the idea that maybe the reason people have gone down to the river with their sweethearts for so long that it's become cheesy is because watching the river really *is* romantic, maybe the river really *does* renew and humble you, maybe love still exists and standing by the river with someone you care about allows you to float out toward the deep seas where it gathers. I let myself give in and be unironically happy. We kissed for half an hour, ears and nose and eyes and chin and tongue—the best kiss I've ever had. My stomach hurts when I think about it.

See, unlike with Mom, when I think about Yegal, it's all happy memories. I'd be in better shape if I could dislike him. Two months ago, when he took off, I was getting close to finishing a new painting called *Flight*. I told him about it during our goodbye. He said if I ever wanted an outside eye, he'd love to take a look at it for me. So a week and a half later, I mailed it to him in Vermont. We hadn't spoken since he left, but I assumed that this was because he was settling in, setting up shop, figuring out how to adjust his habits to this new place. I thought it would be sweet, that he'd be touched to get the painting itself instead of just a slide. I thought he was probably lonely and this would make him feel loved. I basically thought that, maybe, he'd care. But I never heard from him. For a while, I called and left messages at the colony's office, but he never got them, or if he did, I wasn't important enough for him to bother calling back. I imagined taking the bus up to Vermont and demanding he give my painting back. Stupid idea, of course, since he was only there for five weeks and by now he's gone off somewhere else. Probably sitting in some Starbucks with a new student, drinking ginseng tea and whispering aesthetic theories into her ear. It's really a compulsion, isn't it, making up present-tense lives for the people who've left you behind? I can just hear him complaining about the conceptual stuff coming out of England, his clothes smelling spicy, like turmeric, because he hasn't washed them in two months, his head tilting and his brow tightening as he nods and frowns, pretending to listen to the flow of his new student's childish thoughts.

His last night here, when we said goodbye at his apartment, I asked if I could sleep over. Not to do anything, just to hold him, because I was going to miss him. He blushed. He couldn't look at me while he explained what a bad idea he thought this was. "Afraid you won't be able to control yourself?" I teased him. "Hah, I'm afraid *you* won't be able to control *yourself*." I crawled over his stomach, kissed him and said, "I can take care of me." He whispered in my ear, "No. You can't. But I can't take care of you either." I pretended not to hear this. Then he flicked his tongue around the crevices of my ear and we messed around on the floor for a while, slowly, both of us timid and overprotective of each other. It was like we were swimming; we'd press toward each other with great bursts of energy, and then, when we knew we were both in the same state of excitement, we'd tread water and calm down, catch our breaths and make sure we could still see the shore. I can't believe I actually did this, but I could tell that there was no way he'd break the rule he had for himself, so I grabbed his wrist and placed his hand on my breast. He actually gasped when he touched it. Out loud. I think he was expecting a bra. He got lost there for a few minutes and then he just stopped. "No, I can't do this," he said. "Don't you want to?" "Does it seem like I want to?" "Uh-huh." I arched my eyebrows, trying awkwardly to be flirtatious. "Of course I do." "So?" "It's just . . . I don't want to hurt you." "You won't. I want to, too." "I'm leaving tomorrow." "I know." "And you're only sixteen." "So." He laid his head on the hardwood floor and stared at the ceiling. His whole body was tense. "It's just, I actually like you," he said. "I know," I said, and kissed him and kissed him until he began to respond. For the rest of the night, we pressed further and further across his lines. I tried to make it absolutely clear to him that I understood that we both had big, confusing lives ahead of us and that neither of us was in any position to sacrifice those lives for someone else right now, but I don't think I made this sufficiently clear to myself. I believed it while I was saying it, but I think I mostly just wanted to get him to let me give myself to him. He was careful and tender and kind as he crossed the last line. I told him I loved him and he said, "Don't say that. I want you to love yourself." That's what made me cry.

How far is the furthest you've ever gotten? After long hours of staring at the box, have you ever opened it up and tapped out a blade? Were you worried that you might actually cut yourself? I bet you were. They're not easy to pick up. The impulse is to pinch the two long sharp sides, but you can't, you have to brace your thumb against the lower blades and flick your forefinger across the top of the stack until you've dragged the top blade far enough out to get a grip on the short side—unless you're like me and don't care if you slice your fingertips, physical pain being part of the whole thing. Once you have the blade in your hand, do you admire the compact utilitarian genius of its design? Do you pivot it over a candle so you can study the movement of the gleaming squiggle of light on the steel, wondering at the laws of physics that allow this light to bounce? When I hold a blade like that, I always imagine it's a small but trustworthy shield, that the light's trying to burst past it, trying to sear me, and the blade's my only defense. The blade is cold. It protects me from getting sappy and willing myself to believe things will get better when obviously they won't.

Is your once-acclaimed, ultra-realist eye that clear? It should be, it might toughen you up. Maybe then you could lower the blade to your wrist without trembling and hold it so close to the skin that it feels like it's touching even though it's not, so close that when you breathe deep and your arm slightly lifts, the blade pricks you. That's when you realize what it is you're doing, but you don't draw blood—not yet. What I do is, I apply a fraction of pressure, pressing just a corner into my flesh until a minuscule bead of blood creeps out. I peer at it closely. Sometimes I taste it. Then I imagine what it will look like after I pull the blade down the length of my forearm. The vein will open like a zip-lock bag, the blood tumbling out to the beat of my pulse. To be effective, you can't imitate what you see in the movies. You need to cut lengthwise, not crosswise, and carefully follow the line of the largest vein, five or six inches down each arm. It's called double blue veining. If you cut crosswise, the hole will be small and the blood will clot too quickly, stopping the flow. I imagine watching my blood stream and eddy, my self swim away from myself.

Could you take the next step, Dad, and actually slice? Or would you do what I do: hover with the blade, swiping slowly, scratching deep enough only to tap the extreme surface capillaries and draw dotted lines across the surface of your ambition. What are you afraid of—dying? Not me. I'm afraid of pain. There's a degree of inadvertent pain that I've mastered—cutting my fingertips while my mind's occupied with some mechanical task—maybe removing a razor blade from a box or biting my knuckle until it bleeds while I'm trying to figure out what to do next on a painting—but the sting and throb of opening a vein, the meticulously prolonged act of creating the wound requires more nerve and courage than I've so far been able to muster. I can't imagine it's any worse than how I feel generally, every day. Each time I take a razor blade into my hand, I'm more confident than I was the last time that this will be the day I find out, but I still haven't psyched myself up to the adrenaline peak from which, holding my breath, I can leap and soar away. Not yet. I'm still at the stage where I psyche myself out instead.

You're back in your darkroom. Why is that, Dad? You're thriving. You're working. I saw you today in the park with a girl. You had your old Nikon out. She was laughing. She wasn't much older than me. And you were flashing that sharp, playful look you get when you're lost in your work, when you're captivated and outside yourself. Are you doing heart-work? Have you told her about Mom? Or me? Your red light is on, but I'm stuck out here.

Dad, I wish you'd come out. My sense of purpose is fragmenting now. I'm starting to wallow in the nowhere feeling that always comes over me after I've lost my nerve.

FAILURE TO THRIVE

I like babies. That's why I do what I do. I'm a nurse. I work in the maternity ward. Protect the kids from the goblins and ghouls of the night. I do my job well. I take it seriously. I worry over the little lives in my charge as if they were my own children. I fret for their futures. Some nights while Kim or Cheryl—whichever I'm paired with—is on break, I lean over the babies and listen to their shallow breaths.

Before I get to my job, though, I need to tell you a different story.

While I was in nursing school, I knew a couple who had a baby girl. Her name was Sabrina and I adored her.

Her father had once been a heroin addict. Sick and scared and full of self-loathing, he'd tried to hide this from Sabrina's mother. She knew the signs, though, from the aimless crowd she ran with, ambitionless dreamers, singer-songwriters, poets, bookstore clerks, coffee jerks. He never ate. The dirty, long-sleeved t-shirts he liked to wear were speckled with cigarette holes. When she looked in his eyes, sometimes she couldn't find him inside. His mouth was dry when they kissed and he wasn't interested in having sex. He was often edgy, hands drumming jeans, and late at night he'd suddenly bolt with no explanation. One night when she was feeling especially lonely and weak, she asked him, *Please, stay the night, stay an hour, just fifteen more minutes.* When he said no, she cried and he leapt up from the futon and paced the room, saying *I have to go, don't you get it, I just have to go.* He was sweating. *Fine, go, go shoot up,* she said, and she cringed. In a rush of fury and profanity, he told her that though it was none of her business, yeah, if she cared so much, he did shit sometimes. *So sue me; so kill me; you're the one who's crying.* She didn't spin off into outrage or berate him for hiding and lying, for his sloppy cruelty. She didn't smother his pain in her own. Nor did she threaten to leave him, force a reaction, grab the upper hand. Instead, she waited for him to exhaust himself, then rose from the futon, walked slowly to him and held him. He cried at her touch. They cried together and it was more intimate than anything they could have said right then, even more intimate than sex. They cried for a long time, and once the tears slowed and started to dry, they clung to each other, listening to themselves breathe, deeply, in counterpoint, almost as if they were harmonizing, and that's when she knew he was the man with whom she'd have a child.

From then on, he stayed most nights. She let him fix in the bathroom at first, then right in front of her on the futon, on her bed, behind the locked door of the guest room at her mother's house. Watching him thrilled her. She would've tried it herself, if not for the sad look that fell over his face when she pressed him to describe the feeling—*Tell me in detail, is it as incredible as people say, is it heavenly?* She learned from this look that he wanted her to disapprove, to give him a reason to transcend himself.

Eventually, trailing the phantom of their shared future, he kicked. She didn't pressure him. He went cold turkey and she fed him wonton soup from the corner Chinese while he shivered. Her only demand was that, when the frenzy inside him became too unbearable, he pound bruises onto her chest, hitting her as hard as he could, so she could experience some of his pain.

She reminded him of all this one night years later at a claustrophobic, poorly lit bar. He'd joined NA and done the twelve steps and then stopped going. He didn't need to. He'd lost his passion for everything but her. And in the three years that had passed, though they'd never married, Sabrina was born. Despite this fact—if a child can be called a fact—or maybe because of it, she'd grown bored and resentful toward him.

She told him she hated him. Well, maybe she didn't hate him, but she hated the grind of her life with him. She didn't know how things had gotten to this point—no, she did know, but she couldn't understand why she'd allowed it to happen. This stupid love was more pity than empathy, and cohabitation was merely another addiction, one they now shared without any incentive of satisfaction. He'd been a mystery that, once revealed, turned out to be another sham. It was as if he'd flinched in the midst of drying out and, caught in the shame of self-recognition, seized up. She was annoyed by the care he took in listening to her, the way he slunk off to perform the inane tasks she thought up to get him out of the house and away from her. When they'd met, he'd had strong opinions and passions, zest, verve. He'd been self-centered in all the best ways. But for him the nights of mosh pits and after-hours parties, of body shots with strangers, were gone; that life was gluttonous, dangerous, too likely to be perfumed with temptation. Now he was pinched and terrified, constantly sorry for constantly trying to please her, for handcuffing her to his doting heart. This life was as stupid as the love it had been constructed around. She'd stayed home fretting back when he was running wild and now that he was clean, she still stayed home fretting, over his baby now instead of him. But he'd had his reckless fun, why shouldn't she?

She told him she'd made some decisions. She said, and I paraphrase only slightly, "Look, I'm bored, okay. You go to classes and study and whatever, and I'm stuck in the house like some fucking housewife. I'm twenty-five and I've already got a baby! I shouldn't have a baby yet! I feel like I have to do what my heart says, and my heart says screw it. Explore. Don't be afraid. This ex of mine called me the other day and I met him for coffee. We sort of talked and whatever, and it was nice. It was all still there, you know?"

"Did you sleep with him?" he asked.

"Not yet, but I want to."

"What about me?"

"We're not married."

"But we're committed, aren't we?"

"I think we should have an open relationship."

"What about what I think?"

"You know what? I'm done caring what you think." The muscles along the edge of her mouth flexed and pulsed. "I'm telling you how I *feel*. If you really love me, you'll try to understand and not stop me. And if you don't really love me, then . . ." She shrugged, sighed, and he saw a touch of dread flit through her eyes. "You know what? If I can't explore what's out there, we're doomed. I know. I can feel it. You're not going to try to stop me anyway. You're just going to guilt me. That's how you do things. But you know what? It won't work this time."

"So this is a test?"

"Sure."

"That's cruel."

"I'm not trying to test *you*. I'm trying to test *me*."

"Oh, yeah?"

"Yeah . . . don't be like that. I'd think you, of all people, would understand. I need to . . . I don't know, I feel dead."

He didn't know what to say. He wondered if she was misspeaking, if her problem was more that she felt too alive—stuck in the wrong life—and wanted to kill her current self off so she could start over as someone different. He didn't ask her. He waited in silence for her to elaborate.

"You know, I was just getting into the scene when I met you. You'd done all this shit, and you, like, knew what that world was. But I sort of—"

"What world?"

"That . . . drug world, or whatever you want to call it. Where life's scary enough, real enough, that you have to figure out who you are."

"What do drugs have to do with any of this?"

"I want to know what I'm missing. I've been thinking about heroin, too."

"Where are you going to get that?"

"This ex I had coffee with knows somebody."

Again, he held his tongue.

"I just . . . I want things to be exciting again. Things felt exciting when you were all fucked-up. I mean, here was this big sexy junkie who liked me and I thought, hey, that's cool. But then you tried to protect me from all the dark shit you knew, like you couldn't imagine that maybe I *wanted* to know it, too. That maybe that's what attracted me to you. You know? Maybe I had demons of my own. And then you were trying to clean yourself up, and that was exciting. I got to be like an icon or something, which made me feel sexy, and everything was great. But now, you know, it's boring . . . I'm sick of trying to live up to your expectations. I don't *want* to be perfect. I want to know what's out there."

He wasn't in a position to try to talk her out of anything. It seemed to him that if she was in some sort of pain, it wasn't his place to judge her method of treatment. "What are you going to do with Sabrina while all this stuff is going on?"

"Maybe you could look after her sometimes. No. Fine. I'll leave her with a sitter . . . or if I can't find one, I guess I'll bring her along."

Disturbed, he walked her home.

o   o   o

At that time, I was undergoing a training rotation through the NICU, and while I was there, I helped monitor a premature infant, He'd been born at thirty-one weeks and weighed 1200 grams, so small he could fit into a coffee mug. His skin was translucent and loose on his bones, his fingertips and lips perpetually soft blue. At birth, he'd been outfitted with a monitor to track changes in his heart and respiratory rates. Within his first hour of life, he experienced two episodes of apnea and was diagnosed with respiratory-distress syndrome. A clear plastic hood connected him to a CPAP machine so that oxygen could be pumped into his lungs. He had a one-in-four chance of survival.

It was my job to stroke his small body, to provide the warm contact that's been proven to bolster neonatal growth. I noted changes in his condition and monitored him for responses to the electrolyte solution he was being fed. I examined his papery skin for the white lines, like hairline cracks, that would imply he was malnourished or dehydrated. In some inchoate way, he seemed neither human nor inhuman, like he was teetering on the edge of being, just a hair more sentient than a fetus.

At 7:34 a.m., near the end of the fourteenth hour of his life, his respiratory system began to fail. I was across the room at the time, peering at a different child with the head nurse and two other trainees. His distress was discovered by a sensor connecting his body to a monitor. His chest was at war with the blue machine.

When this third episode of apnea tripped the alarm, the head nurse ran to him, did some quick tests and fiddled with the CPAP's controls. Over her shoulder, I glimpsed him seizing and startling, curling in on himself, but I was quickly pushed back by the doctors who swarmed toward him. I was a peripheral presence, unnecessary, a thin, feeble cloud on the edge of the storm of hands passing equipment and flipping charts and performing operations I had not yet been taught. At the center of all this stood the head nurse, who, as I was told later, was pumping her thumb lightly against his minuscule rib cage. And then it was over. When the doctors dispersed, I went to the child, scooped him up and held him like an offering in two cupped hands. His skin had gone milky white. His veins glowed like coral lit up beneath glass. His oceanic eyes were wide open. His knees were bent, his arms crossed over his heart. He was dead.

I was told that even if he'd been discovered in time, if I'd been there to slow the oxygen, if I'd hooked him up to an ECMO, he'd still have died. He was frail and ill equipped, even for life on a water mattress or in an isolette under bili lights.

The death of this child had an odd effect on me. I found myself lingering over the memory of having held his dead body in my hands. I'd blink and I'd see his blue head, gigantic, almost as big as his torso. I'd blink again, and there would be his eyes, black and deep as the future. I could only half listen at the weekly sharing seminar that Thursday morning. I only half read the handbook that was our vocational bible. I watched without seeing the head nurse's step-by-step tutorial on how to perform an electrocardiogram. The child kept squirming in my head. I wondered if his parents had named him or if he had siblings or if his parents had bought him mobiles and plush blankets and blue stretchies with feet, if they had a crib and a playpen and a changing table set up in a dark alcove of their home, if there was a room they were now afraid to enter. I didn't look for answers to these questions, just let them rattle around in my mind. I lost my appetite. I couldn't sleep.

Almost a week after he died, I was still disturbed. At lunch in the hospital cafeteria with my fellow trainees, I picked at my gluey lasagna and failed to laugh at the intrigues involving spilled bedpans and missing pharmaceuticals that baroquely peppered their gossip. The child had no name. He'd died before his parents had fully imagined him. He was anonymous—Baby Boy, Martin— Patient Number u30.1157204. I christened the dead baby Michael, and having named him, I realized I hadn't been mourning. Not exactly. I'd been brooding, wondering why he'd died and whether he'd chosen this death himself. It seemed quite possible that he'd known where he was, that while in the womb he'd heard the world swarming around him, the footsteps of his father, the heavy sighs of his mother. I wondered if he'd known whose hearth he was crossing, and if it had filled him with dread. I could almost see the place, a blur of green lawn on a treeless plot surrounding a lowly ranch house, the kind that boldly proclaims its allegiance to dreams its inhabitants cannot attain. I could almost see his parents, ineptly striving, I couldn't tell what for, but I saw them frustrated in their attempts. I could almost see Michael desperately trying to flee.

Sabrina's eyes were a pale gray, verging on blue-white like faint clouds that bespeak nothing but beauty on a warm day. When they were open, the lids spread so wide that her corneas seemed to be floating in milk; when closed with sleep, they were still partly open, as if she were watching the action around her from behind her bramble of lashes. Her mouth was small and delicate, a mouth made for soft kisses. Her hair was slow to grow, a wisp of down crowning her head like a Mohawk, offering no protection. She already knew five words. She liked to wear hats, floppy fisherman's caps, gnomic thermalwear with earflaps that could be tied under her chin, anything with loose parts that she could yank down. "Saf, saf," she would say. She liked to be covered. She had learned to stand early, and though she wobbled, her legs rarely buckled. By lunging from the arm of a chair to the edge of a coffee table to the seat of the couch to the TV set, she was able to maneuver through any room, grabbing pens and coins, paper clips, dust bunnies, remote controls, anything meant for adults, anything but her own toys, to jam in her mouth and gnaw on, to drop, to throw, to pound and scrape surfaces with, or to place nicely, with a coy smile and the word "nut," the opposite of "yed," into a parent's hand. She hated shoes but loved socks. Her father would slip her socks onto her feet and she would erupt in giggles. "Saf, saf, saf." Her father thought this meant safe. She seemed to say it most while being dressed. It wasn't until she pulled the neighbors' cat's tail that he understood it meant "soft." Sabrina was smart for her age and cute for her age and big for her age. A precious child. I thought so, anyway.

She knew two other words. "Day-yay" was "Daddy." "Mumum" was "Mom." And I think she knew things about these two people that she couldn't express with words. Day-yay liked to play Where's Sabrina while he was dressing her. He liked to play Little Piggy. He liked to play Got Your Nose. Lots of times, Day-yay wasn't home; he was away at school learning how to be a grown-up. Mumum took Sabrina for rides in the car sometimes in the middle of the afternoon; sometimes Mumum cried before these rides. One time Sabrina screamed "Mumum" over and over as loud as she could and Mumum forgot to answer even though she was sitting right there with her eyes open. Day-yay loved Mumum, but he was afraid to talk to her unless she started talking first. I think she knew all this. I believe these were her thoughts.

I studied the children in Intensive Care more carefully now. They had slow heartbeats, blue fingers and toes, sluggish—sometimes nonexistent—responses to the doctors' slaps and prods, low birth weights, malfunctioning internal organs. They were born with port-wine stains on their shoulders, strawberry marks across their faces, swollen eyes leaking pale yellow pus. This one had thrush. This one had jaundice. This one did not have a startle reflex. Sometimes the only thing wrong with them was that they just wouldn't grow— failure to thrive, it's called—and I found these to be the most disturbing; I wondered if, maybe, they were rebelling, psychosomatically saying No as they tried to crawl after Michael.

According to their corrected ages, the preemies were each minus zero; sometimes minus one month, sometimes three, none of them were born yet. They were here, they were out, but they

were still gestating. I wondered who would be the next to fail to survive, and if this could truly be called a failure. Maybe, until they
were zero years old, the preemies were not yet fully alive and
though they were out in the world, breathing through machines,
eating through plastic tubes, their beings, their essences, whatever
it was that constituted their incorporeal parts, were as unprepared
for life as their bodies were. And maybe, because they were younger
than the youngest baby, they were also older than the oldest septu-
agenarian—the aged always look like infants. Maybe they were
ageless, and from this vantage they could see their futures and
choose to accept or reject them. Maybe those whose bodies
stopped pressing toward life were opting out while they still had a
choice.

And maybe that glimpse I'd had in the cafeteria of Michael's
future was more than my imagination. Maybe I saw what he'd seen,
or a portion of it. Maybe he'd meant for me to see the sadness his
life had promised him. Why? To what end? To make me a better
nurse, I thought.

I searched the preemies for glimmers of personality, for visions
similar to those Michael had shown me, but I saw nothing. Life
begins when the spirit inhabits the body, when the body is able to
survive and thrive on its own, with the help of its nurturing parents.
Science was keeping these bodies going, and I believe their spirits
still hovered on the hand of God, a perch from which they could
see me searching for them. So they hid. They still weren't sure if
they wanted the lives these bodies would give them. Their pain still
floated in the what-might-be and they didn't need me to see the
what-will-be. They could take care of themselves.

I wish now that I'd paid more attention to the full-term babies.
They might've been more communicative. I try to remind myself
that the ailments they suffered were physical, and that I'm more
concerned with the bloodless ruptures, the spiritual ailments, in
my patients' lives. I try to convince myself that the distressed bodies
of the full-term babies in the NICU will ensure that they are

attended to, cared for and comforted throughout their lives, but I know this isn't true. There must have been one, at least one, for whom I could have done good. Even the physically handicapped fall prey to shattering sadness. Even the kid with the hole in his heart might one day find that heart too heavy. At the time, though, I still didn't understand my calling.

Sabrina's father began to have trouble accessing his emotions—he knew they were inside him, even knew which ones he needed to feel, but they wouldn't come out. He was so alone that even his own feelings refused his company. He wandered with plodding steps, like a nomad, across the cracked earth of his home. The way he described it, his bones felt like they'd been emptied of marrow, the blood in his veins as thick and rank and slow-moving as sewage. It took all of his effort to form the simplest thoughts: *change the baby; feed the baby; rise above yourself and play with the baby now.*

Time moved so slowly. There was too much of it. Sabrina's mother came home sporadically. He couldn't tell her to change her lifestyle. He couldn't tell her anything. She'd put up with him, and now it was his turn to put up with her. Already she claimed it was unfair for him to demand that the changes she was making stay outside the house. "When did you get to be so high and mighty?" she said. When he tried to explain it wasn't for his sake, but for Sabrina's, she wouldn't listen. He had no credibility.

Sometimes she took Sabrina out with her—he'd come home from school and find the house empty. Then time stopped moving completely. He lay on the futon staring at nothing, thinking of nothing, becoming as close to nothing as he could, waiting for time to move again or, if not that, to end altogether.

He knew he'd eventually get past this numbness. Something would happen, then time would speed up and crash into his emotions, knocking them loose, maybe shattering them. The emptiness wouldn't matter as much if he could have Sabrina with him, if he could carry her everywhere on his hip, if he could always be sure she was okay.

After my stint in the NICU I was rotated to the maternity ward, where I eventually was given a full-time job. I worked there until yesterday. The maternity ward differed from the NICU in a variety of ways, chiefly in that the babies there had passed their Apgar tests, which meant they were healthy, physically prepared to thrive in the world. Three of us, Kim and Cheryl and I, worked two at a time in staggered night shifts.

Cheryl was older, in her late forties. She was a light-skinned black woman, with freckles that rose from her cheeks, and was deeply involved with the Jehovah's Witnesses. She never slouched, and her head rode high on her neck like that of a teacher obsessed with discipline. Her personality was like her posture, strong-willed, rigid and certain. She impressed and intimidated me. She had none of the cracks that I connect with in people, nor did she abide these cracks in others. In my first few days she seemed to take glee in correcting me, mostly about minute procedural details. *When you burp the children, you fold the towel like this, not like that, you don't want gunk all over your scrubs. Throw the wet wipe out immediately, don't put it in your pocket and spread germs around to the other children, we can't have that.* Part of me aspired to be more like her, to be convinced of the rightness of my methods, but another part of me wished she'd just leave me alone.

Kim had boyfriend problems and a cigarette addiction. She exhausted me. She spent most of her time in the windowed room off the nursery, listening to her Walkman and leafing through the new issues of the complimentary magazines, *People* and *Parenting* and *Cosmopolitan*, even *GQ* and *Sports Illustrated*, using them up before dropping them back into the Formica cubes in the waiting room. I minded this less than when she chose to talk to me; then the air thinned out, and I suffered from lack of oxygen and vertigo.

The topic was almost always the same: she wanted advice on her boyfriend, but if she got it, she'd decide the advice was wrong.

I kept my distance from both of them and gave my attention to the babies. At this age they were all the same, barely sentient lumps of flesh, covered in vernix caseosa and a downy layer of lanugo, needing almost nothing, only food, warmth. Each started wet and, while drying out, slowly solidified. They burped up mucus and embryonic fluids. They leaked sludge-like meconium into their diapers. Their bodies made so many after-the-fact preparations. The points at the top of their heads receded. Their skin darkened and thickened, eye color deepened, noses and ears changed shape, firmed up, realigned. They hardened as their bodies primed for the future, and if they'd been seals or fawns or kittens this would've been enough; but they were born human and as such they'd eventually start asking questions that had no answers, searching for patterns that didn't exist, falling prey to dangers of their own creation, from which instinct could not protect them. They slept and slept and slept, and upon waking, they tired quickly, fleeing back to sleep after five minutes of consciousness.

Most mothers roomed in. They had rooms with windows and flowers and mounted TVs, with collapsible curtains that could be unfurled for privacy while they nursed. They planned ahead and made various demands: no pacifiers, no bottles, hard-to-come-by foods and visiting rights for their extended families, no nurses. Their babies were the culmination of long-held dreams. But the children in the nursery had problems. They were the children of frail, wealthy women in need of extra recovery time, or poor women there without family, or women whose husbands were out at the bar, whose boyfriends were in jail, whose handful of lovers had no idea—and never would—that they'd just given birth; these were the children of children who would never see them, of women who would never want them, of parents already beginning to feel guilty for being less capable than they knew they should be.

I wondered how healthy these babies really were. Physically, yes, they were fine, but that was small comfort. Only a few hours out of the womb and already they were deficient. For a host of reasons, their lives were already difficult. This one bawled when his arms were trapped in his swaddling blanket. This one had two pre-teeth wobbling in her gums, abrading them, causing soreness and bleeding and unending agony. This one blinked so slowly it seemed that the world might end before she next batted a lash. This one wouldn't take a bottle. This one didn't cry. Already, they were individuals.

They made me sad. I mixed their formula. I stuck thermometers into their armpits. On my rounds I tried to treat them tenderly, but I felt like a fraud; with every kind act I promised a lie, set an impossible precedent. What happened after they were taken home was out of my control. The temperature would no longer be fixed at a constant 65°. The length of the day would no longer be decided by the rheostat. The institutional stability of the hospital would be replaced by messier, less controllable circumstances.

For a stretch there, Sabrina refused to eat. She had constant colic, screaming and squirming and shaking, her whole body quivering, skin blushing with so much blood it looked like it might pop. Her parents were frightened. She lost weight and they worried that she would suffer irreversible damage if she didn't start to eat again soon. She might die of malnutrition. I think she was frightened, too. I think she was disappointed by what she'd encountered on this side of the birth canal and was refusing to grow. I think she was looking for mercy. As she howled, she turned to face the sun and raising her palms, she begged for deliverance, for release, for eternal returns.

Some nights, when I was restless and done with my chores, I trolled the aisles between bassinets and watched the babies sleep. I paused over each child, prayed for him or her. I was all that stood between them and the wild and I was not enough. Within a few days they'd be out in the world. They'd be on their own, at their parents' mercy, and forever after they'd have to struggle for the simple things I provided them with. Two arms around them. A purr in the ear. The nudge of a nose on the cheek. Undivided attention.

On one of these nights, I found myself returning over and over to a particularly frail, small, dark-skinned boy. He was marked with a nevus high on his left cheek. His face twitched as he slept and he kept waking up. I held him on my lap, bouncing and rocking him for most of the night, but it didn't help.

I was on with Kim that night, and the noise annoyed her. "I don't know why we can't sedate them when they get like this," she said.

"Why don't you go smoke a cigarette?" I snapped.

On her way out, she rubbed the boy's head. "Poor baby," she said and he started to wail. She waved him off and kept walking. "Fine, be like that," she said.

When she was gone, he calmed down. He gazed at me— oddly, urgently. I kissed his forehead. We were sitting in the shadows of the unlit nursery, and I saw something dance in the space between his face and mine. A darkness on top of the darkness. I couldn't make out what it was, but I had a sense of what I couldn't see. The arc of his life. Any happiness it contained would be secondhand, stories he'd tell himself after the fact. Happiness is what he would call those moments that, when he remembered them, seemed less sad in contrast to the rest. I grabbed a blank chart and jotted down some notes.

Jones, BB
u32.3691550

He will be miserable most of his life, and when he's an old man he'll curse having ever been happy.

I knew what I'd written was true. I wished there was some way to cure him of it.

I managed to get him back to sleep before Kim returned, and I laid him gently into his bassinet.

"All better?"

I nodded, averting my eyes, and busied myself disinfecting bottles as she lingered, hoping for small talk.

"You don't have to do that right now," she said.

"I know."

"You want anything from the candy machine?"

I shrugged and she left again.

The scalding water focused my mind. Why hadn't the Jones boy, like little Michael, chosen to flee from his future? I tried to work out the metaphysics. As long as he was in his mother's womb, his body was controlled by hers. Michael had a choice because, as a preemie, the normal birth process had been disrupted; his mother had relinquished his body before the groundbreaking due date at which he would have begun to forget the life of which he'd seen the outlines; in this window of time, he'd had the chance to abort the project. The Jones boy did not have this option. Now that he was out, the process of forgetting was in full swing. His urgent gaze had been a plea for help, a last look around before he succumbed to the tedium of time, the inevitable life ahead of him.

I was off the next night, but stopped by anyway just to check in. It was early, around nine-thirty, and Kim was on dinner break.

Cheryl, alone in the nurses' station, hovered over the study guide she worked on every night at about that time. "You're not supposed to be here," she said.

"Just picking up my pay stub."

"Payday was yesterday."

"Yeah, I forgot."

She peered at me skeptically, as if over glasses, though she didn't wear any.

I rubbed my knuckle in circles along the long table mounted into the wall. I was tired. I hadn't slept well that morning—thinking about the Jones boy—and didn't have the energy to bulwark myself against her prodding. "How are you?" I asked, looking her directly in the eye, something I almost never did.

"Um . . ." She weighed her answer and for a second her eyes lost their ferocity. "Okay."

I'd never before seen her show any weakness. "You sure?"

She readjusted her perfect posture. "I'm well, yourself?"

I shrugged.

"Listen, are you going to be here for a second? I've got to make a phone call."

"You sure you're okay?"

"Yes. I . . . I should call my son, though."

I agreed to cover for her and she ran down the hall to the pay phone. It rattled me to think that not even Cheryl could shut the turbulence out of her life.

While she was gone, I trolled the aisles and found the Jones boy. It pleased me that he was still there. He was the reason I'd come, really. I picked him up. I put him down. He was sleeping peacefully, finally.

I stared at my reflection in the window of the nurses' station while waiting for Cheryl to return. I looked gaunt. I could see my skull through my skin. I wondered how many years I had left to live.

When Cheryl got back, she was again impenetrable and stern. "Everything quiet?"

"Yeah, it's quiet," I said, and I left.

One night, Sabrina and her mother didn't come home at all. They didn't come home the next night, either. Nor the next, nor the next. They never came home again. I have no idea where they went. Her father did nothing to find them. He just let them go.

It was almost a year before another child showed himself to me. In that time, Kim married her problem boyfriend. Cheryl tried to convert me and, having failed, she now kept her distance. I had attempted to reach a variety of children the way I'd reached Michael and the Jones boy, and couldn't understand why they didn't respond. My only thought was that it wasn't up to me. I was merely their receptacle. All I could do was be ready, poised and present, the next time one of them needed me.

And I was. When the little girl with the twitching feet gazed up at me from the changing table, when I saw those urgent eyes, I grabbed the chart I'd reserved for this moment and scribbled down what they were saying. It was like taking dictation:

Swenson, BG
u32.3691497

One week, her fear will reach such a pitch that it will keep her awake for one hundred and twenty straight hours. Nights, she'll lie on the cot, beneath the thin moth-eaten blanket and contemplate the signs and symbols that seem to be rushing not through her mind but through the room itself. She'll be convinced that if she can discern the exact meaning of her visions, she will not only have uncovered an essential truth, but will also be allowed to exit this place, to return to her mom and dad, return to the girl she once was— the one whose smile alarmed people with its sincerity, whose precocious mind made connections that widened the eyes of the adults around her, whose heart was so immense and trusting that every day, even long after she should've known better, she willingly gave her bag lunch away to the school bully, happy to help make him happy. Her visions—bright

*lights that murmur words she can't make out, the Book of
Isaiah burning, as she reads from the thin pages of her
Bible, the wounds only she can see on the other innocents
locked with their wild imaginations into the ward—will
slowly begin to accumulate resonance. She'll begin to
understand. She'll search for words that might explain what
she's uncovered, words the doctors won't be able to dismiss or
twist, as they're wont to do, into mocking, damning questions. Late on the night of her fifth day without sleep, she'll
find it, a single word, all that the world needs to hear:
Mercy. She'll sob quietly, and when she peeks over the edge
of the blanket she will see that three men dressed in white are
climbing silently into the room through the barred sixth-
floor window. For a moment she will believe they have come
to let her out, but when they lean over her, she'll see the pun-
ishing threat in the downward cast of their lips. She'll be so
afraid that her body will cramp. She'll open her mouth to
scream, but she will have no voice. The men will watch over
her, just for a moment, and then fly back out the window. In
the morning she'll remember, Mercy, but she will have forgotten its meaning.*

Then I returned to wiping her bottom and pinning her up.
I kissed her forehead as I placed her in her bassinet. I prayed
with her.

Over the next few years others searched me out—not often,
once every nine or ten months or so. They always waited until
Cheryl or Kim was on break. I did what they asked, recorded their
futures, and prayed with them. I won't list them here, but I've kept
all the charts on which I logged their futures at home in a three-
ring binder. You can read them if that's what you want.

The most recent one found me yesterday. She had a tiny, dime-
shaped mouth, her lips pursed as if they were made for kissing. She

reminded me of Sabrina when she was first born. Large, big hands and feet, but a small mouth. I cried as I wrote down the things she showed me.

Imbrodicci, BG
u32.3691409

He'll never look her up but she will have a photo she's secretly lifted from the album her mother keeps hidden behind the hatboxes and shoe boxes and all the other boxes filled with less meaningful junk under the bed. On days when her mother seems happy, the girl will venture to ask what he was like. Please tell me something about the good times before I was born. *She'll take mental notes on her mother's tales: the sheepish turn of his smile after some unusual, loving words had slipped out of his mouth; his adoration of certain paintings and films, the way he talked about them so late into the night that Mom's eyes did loop-de-loops just to stay open, but he'd keep going, as if the works of art were his lovers and he needed to examine every single one of their astounding traits, staring off at some wide arcadia and then kissing her like she herself was profound. Other times, her mother will evoke a more cunning man, calling him* That bastard who wrecked my life, *leading the girl to see herself as a burden. And there will be worse times, her mother ranting so virulently that the girl locks herself into her bedroom and stares at the photo, imagining a truth her mother's too bitter to see. At these times she'll be Daddy's girl, and nothing will ever compare to his love.*

I kissed the girl on the forehead and prayed with her. Then I looked up and saw Kim. She must've forgotten her Walkman there in the room. She was screaming, *Don't! Don't! Get away from that child!* But she wasn't trying to stop me. Instead, she called security.

Later, I reread what I'd written about the girl and realized what must have happened. I'd lost my empathy. I had grown selfish. The children would never trust me again, and my career was over. This is why Kim had walked in at that moment. I couldn't see the girl in what I'd written, only Sabrina—and not even Sabrina, really, her mother and father, and me, all of us, failing to thrive.

This is what I will say in my defense:

Each individual child arrived into a unique set of circumstances with unique characteristics that I was able to survey. Their minds were already searching for meaning in the world around them—the sweet ammonia smell, the nubby cotton blankets, the cool Plexiglas of the bassinets, the mass-produced, disposable tools of the health-care industry. Still, they lacked so much, wanted so much, needed so much more than their lives would yield, that these few hours with me in the nursery were as good as their lives were going to get. Life is a long rope of crises that yanks at your neck until you're airborne. At the other end of each child's rope, the platitudes Happiness, Peace and Well-being were waiting to mock and badger them, to spit in their faces, to stand always just out of reach. They'd learn this soon, or maybe they wouldn't; some good things might happen to them, but these good things would be the exceptions. Mostly they would endure, they'd cope, they'd muddle through and, if they were lucky, they'd learn not to cry.

Their lives would begin diminishing soon. They'd never again be as safe as they were here, three or four hours old, in the maternity ward. I wanted what was lacking in life—in their lives as well as in mine—to present itself to them, to become more real than the alloys and plastics that surrounded them here. I wanted to bring them closer to God.

This is why—with more tenderness, more love than their lives were prepared to offer them—I held these children in my arms. I ran my fingers across their soft skulls. I kissed them on the forehead.

I mixed their formula and heated their bottles, testing each one on my wrist. I fed them, watching their sweet faces suck at the nipple and flush with contentment and warmth. They were safe with me. I gave them what all children need: empathy, shelter, something warm to eat. Then, when they were full and falling asleep in their cribs, I gave the worst off among them, the one, every few months, with eyes that foretold the most hopeless future, a greater gift. Lifting the chosen one's head from the pillow and again kissing him on the forehead, I let my hand slide over his nose and mouth. I pinched his nostrils. I stopped his breath. I smuggled the child away from the rubble and handed him back to Heaven, where I knew he'd be treated well.

Sometimes, of course, it was a baby girl. After the last breath fled from her body, I lifted my hand from her nostrils and closed her eyes. I knelt beside the crib and prayed for her. I know what I did was right and just, that what I did was kind.

I saved fourteen in all. Each one died smiling. Their sadness was gone, replaced by this expression of thanks.

THE AGE OF MAN

Jason and Billy discovering everything out there: fossils and physics, the layers of history under the ground, the light-years of space in the sky, the past and the future, embedded between them, the present—Jason's and Billy's two separate presents, which no longer contain each other.

The elephant stands all alone at the edge of the pool. It's two in the morning, cloudy and dark, and the surface doesn't glisten. The elephant can't see itself in the water. "Jason won't come back, and Billy can't find me without him." The water is a darker spot in the darkness. The elephant dives in and can't get back out. It struggles and, struggling, sinks deeper.

Jason and Billy discovering summer, until with a backfire, a puff of smoke, it's gone.

The elephant drowns without leaving a trace.

Dragons are pests. They eat the strawberries.

When a human being throws a rock and that rock hits a duckling, the duckling's mother has no choice. People are dangerous. Ducks are our prey. She must kill her maimed child and keep her flock strong. She must do what has to be done. But she needn't mourn. Ducks know no emotion; they live their lives purely on instinct.

Jason's a grown-up now, being one thing and another, thinking of Billy sometimes with a smile, wondering "What ever happened to Billy?" imagining him holed up in a museum, or out in the scorching sun, swatting mosquitoes, shoveling dirt, searching for the missing link. Jason's close to the truth, but he doesn't quite have it right. In his early twenties, Billy, for reasons that have little to do with Jason but a lot to do with magic, remembered a time when he'd been impressed by what he found embedded in the lower strata. He dug deep into the past and tried to retrieve the sensations buried there. He knew no one else had taken them, but when he arrived, they were missing and he felt he couldn't return home without them. Instead, he crossed the highway—a different highway than Jason had crossed. Jason is still here. When Billy reached the other side, he disappeared.

Acknowledgments

Thanks to Richard Abate, Betsy O'Brien, Kate Lee, Gary Fisketjon and Amber Qureshi for help in the publication of this book; to Elizabeth Taylor at the *Chicago Tribune*, Alice Turner at *Playboy* and David Knowles at Ledig House; to Connie, Deb and Jan in the office; to Mike Heppner, Hanvey Hsiung, Oscar Casares, Tommy O'Malley, Nick Arvin, Jeremy Mullem, John Murray, Nick Fracaro and Gabrielle Schaffer, Shelley Stenhouse, Meredith Goldburg, Alice Gordon and Rob Casper for support, both moral and otherwise, in the writing of these stories; to Frank Conroy, the James Michener Foundation and the Copernicus Society of America for their generous sponsorship by way of a James Michener–Paul Engle Fellowship, and to others too numerous to mention here.

Thanks especially to James Alan McPherson, Jodi, Papa Mike, Mom and Dad, for reasons I can't begin to describe.